JOURNEY TO THE EDGE OF LIFE

JOURNEY TO THE EDGE OF LIFE

Tezer Özlü

Translated from the Turkish by
Maureen Freely

TRANSIT BOOKS

Published by Transit Books
1250 Addison St #103, Berkeley, CA 94702
www.transitbooks.org

© Tezer Özlü, 1984
English translation copyright © Maureen Freely, 2025
ISBN: 9798893380002 (paperback)
Cover design by Sarah Schulte | Typesetting by Transit Books
Printed in the United States of America

9 8 7 6 5 4 3 2 1

NATIONAL ENDOWMENT for the ARTS
arts.gov

This project is supported in part by a grant from the National Endowment for the Arts.

All rights reserved. This book or any portion thereof may not be reproduced or used in any manner whatsoever without the express written permission of the publisher except for the use of brief quotations in a book review.

Introduction

Throughout my life it has been from the dead I've drawn my courage. The dead in whose stories I have lived. The dead who succeeded in turning this world of damnation into one where it became possible to live. The dead who in their writings gave us everything in this world we could ever need.

When she wrote these words, Tezer Özlü was not speaking metaphorically. She was telling the blunt truth about her lifelong struggle with life itself. Born into a family whose every ritual was in fealty to the Turkish Republic, and just as strictly schooled by Austrian nuns, she came early to the idea that she was a prisoner of her own body, with suicide her only escape. Having survived the psychiatric ward to which her first attempt consigned her, she found her only solace in the authors who brought her news from elsewhere.

INTRODUCTION

Her brother was already at university, and already writing. His shelves at home were lined with books that she borrowed without his permission. Without waiting for an invitation, she and her best friend took to climbing the dark, dank lanes of Galata after school to eat cakes at Baylan, the Greek patisserie where her brother gathered with other young writers to share ideas. The girls would sit at a neighboring table and listen in, until at last they were invited over. Soon Tezer was skipping school to spend her nights as well as her afternoons in Istanbul's bohemian enclave. By eighteen she was hitchhiking around Europe, having decided by now that she could learn far more from the books she found along the way than she ever could in a classroom. Most were in German, and because many of these were in translation, her reading continued to take her across borders both geographical and artistic. If the stories she began to publish on returning to Turkey defied its cultural conventions, crashing through them like so many sheets of glass, it was thanks in large part to the authors who had slipped into her life from other languages, to point the way.

It is with *Cold Nights of Childhood*, her autobiographical first novel, that she sets out on her own path, on her own terms. As brutally direct as she is when describing her various incarcerations, she bears no ill will toward the homes, marriages, and hospitals that she has by now put behind her. But she has made herself a promise: never again will she set foot in another psychiatric ward. As she sets off down the beautiful road she sees before her, she vows to live by her own lights and write by them.

INTRODUCTION

No matter how high she flies or how low she sinks, she will stay free.

In the summer of 1982—two years after publishing *Cold Nights of Childhood*—she is in Berlin on a fellowship, and still honoring her vow, though she cannot bear the solitude and is hardly able to sleep or eat. As always, she is finding comfort and consolation in books, until one afternoon she picks up a biography of Pavese, the author she reveres above all others—and happens onto a sentence that sends her into an existential tailspin.

They have (almost) the same birthday, she discovers. There are, she calculates, seven years between her birth and his suicide. She does not go on to say that she is (almost) the same age as he was when he booked himself into a hotel room, lay down fully dressed, and swallowed twenty-two sleeping pills. Nor does she ask what pushed him over the edge and might one day do the same to her. But the unasked questions cast shadows over her every sentence, so powerfully felt that she sees no need to explain why she must leave Berlin at once for Prague, why Vienna must be her next destination, why she must just as suddenly leave that city with a friend heading for Istanbul, or why she must then abandon his car near the Bulgarian border to travel westward, first to Trieste, and then to Turin.

All along the way she gives herself over to the forever receding landscapes as she moves forward to her dreaded final destination—the endpoint of Pavese's life, and the edge of hers. But in this recounting, the outside world matters only to the extent that it impinges on her thoughts. For what she is now mapping are the wild landscapes of her mind. Plunging from ecstasy into anguish, and from gentle reflection into furious self-defense, always exhausted but never flagging in her effort to record her every thought, memory, and image in order of their arrival. Taking comfort from the mostly nameless men who briefly loom into view before fading away. Never forgetting the three dead men—Kafka, Svevo, and Pavese—whose writings gave her the strength to live and love. And never, ever apologizing for being the woman she is still in the process of discovering.

The German version of this book was entitled *Auf dem Spur eines Selbstmords* (*On the Trail of a Suicide*). Only after it won the 1983 Marburg Literature Award did she take it into Turkish, refashioning and reordering the text as she went, and giving it a new title that took the emphasis away from Pavese's death and returned it to her own urgent will to live. She was not to know that she would die of breast cancer just two years after its publication. But it has been impossible since then to read her last words without embracing their deadly importance. Prized to this day in the country of her birth as a radical act of liberation, *Journey to the Edge of Life* has never been out of print.

—*Maureen Freely*

JOURNEY TO THE EDGE OF LIFE

I

A moment arrives on that beautiful spring day I spend reading *An Absurd Vice*, a moment when time stops for an hour or eternity while a chill runs through me. To think I was born on the same day as Pavese. The ninth of September. In my case, just after midnight. But this was midnight in Anatolia. It might not yet have reached midnight in Santo Stefano Belbo. Still, we were born on the same day. If not the same year. Seven years separating my birth year and the year of his suicide. What is it that keeps me returning to Pavese in this place. What lifts away time is what binds us together. Wasn't I always reading him in Istanbul. My every heartbeat, and every sight that has ever caught my eye: if ever I can make sense of them, it is through the images he sketches and the phrases he shapes and the words I take from him and make my own. Why. What is it in my nature that drives me to draw him so deep inside.

"Every road has a very precise trait," he says. "Every hill has a human personality."[1]

Didn't that same thought come to you on your first day in Nice, a day in May like any other, when you walked the boulevards, from one to the next, in search of the Mediterranean. Every home or edifice you passed, every window, open or shut. You imagined your way inside. Inventing stories with unconscionable speed, stories that did not belong to you and so followed their own logic, keeping pace with your footsteps as you walked down one boulevard after another, following your creations through solitude, old age, and death, privations suffered, happiness pursued. Reading the names of each house and avenue. All those images of Genoa, still stored in your mind. The day still living inside you, when you ran out of steam and gave up on finding the Mediterranean, when instead you walked down one gray street after another, choked by exhaust fumes, reading the graffiti, thinking how very much this place reminded you of Istanbul. Genoa. It took you back to Galata, to those dark and rainy winter mornings when the wind blew in from the south, and those spring days and autumn days when you wished the wind could lift you up and carry you away, far from that street in Galata where your school's dark corridors awaited.

How well you remember that city now. That city where you tried so hard to find a good hotel, it's as if you were still there. Hotels whose splendid facades belie the fug of neglect inside. An elderly receptionist shuffles down a dimly lit hallway that has never seen summer. Within a cloud of cologne, the old man takes shape. Outside it's hot. Inside, it stinks of mildew. And damp. With every step you take, the stench is worse. It grows and grows. The old man asks for your passport. He writes down your name. Has you sign beneath it. You've given up now on finding anywhere better. Resigned to this city where you can find neither the Mediterranean nor a good hotel. He'll take you upstairs now. Usher you into a lift, perhaps. Take you to a little room beneath the stairs and leave you to yourself. You stayed in that sort of hotel that night. Listening to the coughs and footsteps of people you couldn't see. Now and again, a snatch of conversation, perhaps. There in that room where you tried to get some sleep, in the humid solitude of a Mediterranean city where you never found the sea.

You were lonelier than the whole city. Lonely as an ocean. On your way back to the hotel, you sat down in a café at a crossroads. Do you remember what you drank. Beer. Campari. The avenue lit by streetlamps. A bus stopping just opposite. A football team filing out. You watched them. Then you went on to a bar, the sort of bar where young laborers and apprentices go on a Saturday evening. Some will be playing foosball, perhaps. The graffiti in this city might be in a language you don't know, but you know what these words mean nonetheless. Huge letters on old and dirty walls.

You woke up and it was Sunday morning. The room had still not cooled down. Perhaps it didn't know how to cool down, would never cool down, would forever carry inside it all the sun and heat it had absorbed over the years. You got yourself a coffee, and from there it was a quick walk to the station. One of your favorites, it turns out. In the desolation of a Sunday morning, you took your bags and found your platform. Only for a doll peddler to come wheeling toward you. To tell you he'd been looking for a woman like you all his life. Stay with me, he said. There in Genoa Piazza Principe Station.

What is it that makes you think of that doll peddler for the first time in years as you sit here in Berlin on this, the most beautiful day of spring. And the nights are not enough for me. The days are not enough. Not enough to be human. Words and languages, they can no longer contain me. I go out to the balcony for a moment. Watch the sun struggle to set behind the Berlin skyline. Watch people parking their cars. Their new and brightly colored cars. They park or keep moving. The older I get, the greater the gulf between me and these people in their cars and planes and offices, buses, shops, and streets. It's the same with inanimate objects. Some days I can't even touch a piece of meat. Or those chickens that resemble the carcasses they truly are. I can fry them, but I can't eat them.

I return to past journeys. To the images I brought back with me. I cannot stop.

Yesterday, in Berlin, on that first Sunday in April, I decided to take all the sorrow anything has ever brought me and class it as happiness. Haven't my moments of greatest happiness carried sorrow in equal measure. And beyond them, an expectation. The call of a world I could call my own. An image: I am in my own room drinking my morning tea. That's what I most longed for, those times I spent in mental hospitals—to take my tin cup of tea back to my own room. No one has ever traveled to death as beautifully as you, or so fully alive.

I sat on the balcony for a long time. The balcony of this house on Storkwinkel reminds me of a cell left half-finished. A cell left open to the sky. To the treetops. To trees that are finally shedding their nakedness, bit by bit, with each new day. Sometimes I feel stronger than anyone in the world, but at the same time I feel as bereft as those trees in their unshed nakedness. Especially at those moments when I am no longer myself. Or when two have merged into one. When suddenly a new and alien emotion sweeps through me:

The Taste of Abandonment

It's new to me, this feeling. It has no place in my life or in the world I've built around me. But this was what overtook me as I sat on that cell-like balcony on Storkwinkel, looking up at the sky, as I contemplated those treetops still struggling to shed their nakedness, and a wind rose up from Berlin's abandoned streets to brush against my cheeks.

I stand up. Take a closer look at other houses, other balconies; all are angled so that people cannot see each other. I sit back down on the white sofa. The night is long. Another long day beckons. After sleeping for two hours, I go to Luftbrücke Field. I'll take the same bus back. When the driver takes his break, I step down to wait beside him on the edge of the green and lifeless empty field. It's early in the morning and still cool. Were it not for the fashionable stud sparkling in this bus driver's ear, I would have taken him for a German peasant. And his voice, verging on the erotic as he announces each stop. What a lovely man. At Halensee, when I cross the road in front of the bus, waving him farewell as he waves back, I am struck by the warmth I feel for him, and he for me. In the hours that follow, I keep thinking of this man, driving his bus through the boulevards of Berlin. And I make a decision: suffering and happiness must be one and the same.

Rather than seek to define our surroundings, we must experience them through our senses . . .

When we fall in love, and even if we stay in love, we can already taste the lonely void that the end of love will bring. In much the same way as we can see a clear shape looming through the fog of daily life. The desire for love is every bit as strong as the desire to prove our own existence. There may be people who never see a need to prove their own existence, who have never loved deeply or seen that love turn to pain. They may experience love as love, such people. And intimacy as intimacy, separation as separation, life as life, death as death, and nothing more. And yet life is defined by death, and death by life. But you. For you, separation begins with the first moment of intimacy, just as intimacy begins with the first moment of separation; for you, the first moments of love and tender feeling carry the seeds of their demise. To touch another's skin is to forget your own existence. Or to feel it more deeply. My own existence. Is it not true that every life carries the seeds of its own death.

Boundless longings—they've traveled with me all through life, or should I say, in the midst of life. But the time has come to put an end to tireless searching. The experiences you sought have been experienced. Have been lived out. Some already buried. Turned to earth. So many people who were once so very alive, whose lives were once joined with mine—all gone. In their name, and on their behalf, to miss them, love them. To miss those we love, to long for them—nothing in life can be more important. To miss them and long for them even when they are still beside us. Though we go through most of life alone. While sleeping. While searching for sleep. Even inside the deepest sleep, are there not moments when a person feels the helplessness of solitude. On roads. While reading. While looking out the window at the avenue below. While getting dressed. While undressing. While sitting in a random café, watching random crowds pass by. While looking for nothing. While paying no attention to the people sitting in a random café, because our mind is on something else . . . While trying to remember what moss smells like, while stepping into the street at a crossroads, and remembering at the last moment that we live in a world of cars, while not recognizing a single person in the cafés lining a great boulevard, while wandering through a grocery store, looking for something, anything, to eat, while buying something else from a vendor, thinking lonely thoughts, while missing, loving, being loved by, and making love with those who come and go or leave entirely, and those who die, are born, or grow . . . those who want to live, or do not want to live . . . are we not always alone.

Could a moment ever arrive when I longed for life no longer. Twenty years on, they're playing the same songs. Showing a film made fifty-three years ago. Fashions from the twenties and the fifties in all the shop windows. In the news, it's all famine and war, backward steps and disasters on such an epic scale as to defy the public imagination. Thus life passes us by. You retreat behind your walls. They behind theirs. In another city. Another country. Each to their own country. To speak their own language. Or they try to understand. No two people speak the same language. You understand now that whatever anyone says, they are saying it to themselves. Their every word is in some way an affirmation of self. Even if you're genuinely trying to explain something to someone, you can do no more than express your own view of the world, extol your own wisdom. Every hand that reaches out to caress someone else's body will move across that body as if wishing to caress its own.

This life I thought I could leave feeling fulfilled—now and again it comes to you that the end will come, and still you will be longing for more. As if you'd not yet lived. Is fulfillment even a thing.

As if there is nothing, amongst all the moments we've ever lived, no single moment that our eyes have fully grasped, or our hearts embraced.

What is it that reminds you today, as it does every day, that there is nothing to do in this life, or in the lives passing all around you, nothing to do but wait for death. Life is timeless. Time has no place in it. Childhood, womanhood, manhood, and old age. Life and death. Love and lovelessness. Emptiness and fulfillment—all are intertwined. Reason and madness, existence and the void—they're all of a piece. Like the white nights of northern Europe. Like dawn coming to a sky that never darkened.

You don't write to tell stories. The world is full of stories. Every person's every living day is filled to the brim with them. Nor do I wish to define my surroundings. Even the grayest, emptiest concrete wall is covered with definitions. A single glance suffices. To read everything on that wall. To see children in their gardens, playing amidst the trees, to watch them on the brink of life, to feel a patient's impatience, or the heat of a summer's day, a sky reaching up into infinity, and the shapes of clouds. You close your eyes. You see. You open your eyes. Definitions come undone to lose themselves in the timeless continuum of past, present, and future.

How long can you carry a person like that. Never satisfied. He wears you out. You wear each other out. I took him everywhere with me. From the Bozdağ Mountains of Gölcük, from that little blue lake and the angry grandmother hiding behind the mountains. I took him with me into life's deepest nights and its most distant cities, its youngest loves and earliest mornings. But still, he wanted more.

*In the depths of anguish, there is nothing left for me.
Not even the pride of having faced my loneliness.*

I was young then. I believed there was such a thing as youth. I was happy, I was sad. I took him with me to every town I visited, every street I walked and park I crossed. My companion in every café and inside every building, on every flight of stairs, under clouds and through the wind, in brilliant sunshine and the cold sun of winter. I carried him and watched over him. I sat him down at café tables. Stopped at crossroads to give him a good look at the buildings around us. A very long look. City after city I explored for him, walking their streets and boulevards, observing their people, sharing their winds, nights, and mornings. Watching their autumn clouds change shape and the light break through them. Their hills and stations and seafronts and lovers. Insatiable and ever anxious, I showed him everything I could find on the face of the earth. I tormented him.

Wouldn't let him sleep. Or I sent him plunging into the deep slumber of anguish. I caressed the skin he so hated. I made him chase after experience. Even though I knew he would never savor those experiences as deeply as I did. For there in those streets, squares, stations, airports, harbors, beaches, or darkening skies, there is no life that can answer to my heart's stirrings. Nor could I find the words to express what I felt then. Nothing I saw was enough. Nothing I breathed. Nothing in a wave, or a room, a place, a love. Nothing even in the taste of water. In the days of the week. I forced him to love many bodies. Once, in a metro station, I made him look through the eyes of an old woman. She was mumbling to herself:

"So many centuries, so much coming and going. But still these dark stations are not satisfied, still they yearn for more."

I watched her. Looked into her, through her, to the child in an apple orchard. To the dizzying swings. To a family dining table. To the petty bourgeoisie. Their disagreements. Their struggles. Their sleepless nights. Their deepest slumber. I looked into this woman and saw a lifelong pursuit of connection. Saw a child who had become a woman and remained a woman, never merging with another, complete in herself.

In the lingering dusk of an early summer evening in Berlin, behind three chimneys rising up to the skyline, a warm moon. Between my window and those chimneys, there are rooftops, there are buildings, and the yellow or gray walls of their upper floors. Towering over us all are the treetops, from the unseen streets below comes the never-ending roar of traffic. This is the face of the earth. No need to think about the rest. Nothing in this city to remind you. At least, I have no trouble leaving it behind. All at once, a book title comes to mind: *Tender Is the Night*. The grand rooms of this house. What here could remind you of other houses, other rooms. Berlin's straight walls do not make a night. The walls of Anatolian houses, plaster over wood. Lackluster towns, walls that stop time and speak of childhood fears. Museum walls in the great cities of Europe. Gallery walls. Dead walls. Walls that stifle breath. Are walls life's cemeteries. Are not the selves we parade in the streets all false. Isn't every self that appears on the city streets a new persona, an alibi assumed. Aren't we most ourselves behind the walls. Is it not behind walls that we can best resist the outside world. Put our ears to the wall and listen. This life that never sates us, do we not cherish it inside those walls, whether it breathes or not. I remind him of another poem.

Do not go gentle into that good night.[2]

No other city brings death to mind as much as Berlin does, no other city brings life as much to mind either. Every wall narrow. Every wall closed to the world. Every wall oppresses. I walk through this city carrying all my walls with me. The narrow walls of my parents' house. The smothering walls of marriage. Office walls that stink of cigarettes. The cruel walls of school. The walls of homes and prisons. The walls that served as backdrops for hangings and firing squads. Hospital walls. Madhouse walls, marble walls, shanty walls, the walls of old-age homes, huts, slums, cities, systems. I sit here in the Berlin night and direct Don Giovanni's cries to the sky. In the June twilight. I add mine to his, giving breath to all I've held inside me. Without speaking a word. Can this be the same sky that hangs over every city in the world. Can this really be the same sky that has wrapped itself around the world through the centuries, this world still riven by war and liberation, punishment and injustice, plenitude and hunger, poverty and pain. Night. Soon, very soon, it will descend on all of Berlin's buildings, old and new. Tonight, there will be old women sitting alone in their homes, awaiting death. Tomorrow there will be others sitting alone beneath the trees of city parks, eating ice cream. From the depths of solitude or dementia, they will watch life flow past, signifying nothing. A night that calls out to be embraced. A gentle June evening floats down to the rooftops of Berlin. To this city of splendor. Half East, half West, with Turkey in the middle.

> *All is the same*
> *Time has gone by*
> *Some day you come*
> *Some day you'll die.*
> *Some one has died*
> *long time ago.*[3]

The sun must be somewhere. The only sun we know. But we're not thinking of the sun. Even so, we can feel the heat of a summer that has come early. A gentle heat. And with it, our pain. We're sitting here on a wooden bench beside the ring road. Lanes and lanes of cars roaring past. Being together like this helps us bear our pain. The pain I feel has never been as great as his. Neither of us minds the traffic. The world flowing past us, just half a meter distant, does not concern us. Those noisy and inanely energetic lives and their exhaust fumes. On the ring road, near the Havel Busway. We're just sitting there on our wooden bench. In just another city. At any old time. Our lives erased, no thought for the past or the future. We're living in the moment. Still and silent.

Facing the Sunday traffic. Impervious to the noise. The trees across the way, what world are they shading. These cyclists racing past, what world have they come from and where are they bound. Walking along this same ring road in the rain two days ago, we came upon a tavern called Old Love. A ship. It could have been on the Golden Horn. Dilapidated. Years of accumulated smells. Long years. A woman—huge, fat, and white—behind the bar. The waiter must be her son. His eyes are just like hers.

—How long has this tavern been here. (I ask this right away.)

—Twenty-five years.

No doubt about it, then. This must be Berlin's best-loved tavern. It could be anywhere, in any city where most of the inhabitants are workmen. So this is it. This was where he liked to come and sit whenever he visited this city. Never again. He died two weeks ago. Never again will he look out over the gray waters of the Havel Canal from the tavern called Old Love. The man was ageless. Ageless as death. Never again will he look across the Havel Canal and remember Zoo Station on the day he had to leave.

So here it is, Berlin. Sprawling all around us. Ringed by walls. Ringed by people who are strangers to themselves. Berlin, the loneliest city in the world. Longing. Pain. I can find no other words.

Fine words, suggesting feelings finer still. I return to the wooden bench.

To the warmth of the sun.

I want to take him to Old Love. We're waiting for a bus. But we're waiting for nothing. We're thinking about, talking about, his death. We've taken off our jackets. The heat won't bother us, we think. We can't even feel it. We're sitting in our own slice of time. A slice of time that comes to us like a picture.

Buses roar past us. Turks amongst their passengers, wearing headscarves and pained expressions.

I want to take him to Old Love. As if I'll find him there. He died in a Scandinavian city that has never known the warmth of the sun, where people never look each other in the face. In the city where, one twilit evening, I looked over the rooftops to find the most beautiful red sky. I see him here, at Zoo Station, leaving the city to seek refuge in London. And I see him here, sitting on the windowsill of Old Love, smoking his pipe. Watching the world through his glasses. Thinking all his thoughts at once.

It's the last day of June. It's going to rain again. It's seven minutes to one. The window is open. His photograph on the wall across. Posing before portraits of Kafka and Brecht. On the side wall is a film poster. Black and white. Train tracks. I didn't put it there. It was there when I arrived. I love train tracks. They speak to me of independence, of being free to get up and leave, of never being pinned down. Train tracks promise all manner of independence.

On the side wall, written out in large letters, are my Pavese quotes. So his suicide is here with me.

In my room.

Cohen is singing his songs. On the floor, a picture propped up against the wall. A picture of my Mediterranean, all shadow and sun. Next to this, three photographs of Rulfo. More of him next to my bed. Barely recognizable in one of them. Taken when he was forty-eight years old, but still looking so young. In his other photographs, you see signs of the anxieties he carried into death. Then Frida Kahlo's book.

Two bottles. Mineral water in one of them. I can't say what's in the other.

We're sitting at the edge of the Havel Busway. I want to take him to Old Love. But the bus just won't come. As if there'd be something there to lessen his agony. Or something to cushion it.

Nights and cities come and go. Now it's the "Moonlight" Sonata keeping me company in my room. In two days, he'll leave for Southeast Asia. He'll take his pain with him. He'll find it again in a standard, modern air-conditioned hotel room. Stepping out of the shower, he'll look into the mirror, and into his own catlike eyes. He'll lie down on the bed. He'll miss the other one. The one now buried in southern Germany. Then he'll settle into the warmth of the hotel terrace.

Now it's here, his "Moonlight" Sonata. And we are sitting near the Havel Busway. The sun warms the bond between us. Which is all we have. The bus we take direct to Kantstrasse is crowded. Full of Sunday daytrippers. They're tired, and happy. We're standing.

—He aged fifty years in two weeks. He went into the hospital aged thirty-eight, and he was eighty-eight when he died two weeks later. His eyes so sunken that they melted into the back of his head.

The bus is packed. The bus we'd hoped to take to Old Love didn't stop for us.

We're on the highway now, heading back into the city. Leaving Old Love behind us. The trees and their patches of shade. And now we have the "Moonlight" Sonata. I'll try to get some sleep. Maybe I'll step outside. Maybe. What's Berlin like at two in the morning, I wonder. There will be watchmen guarding your walls. And beyond those walls, Turks asleep in the dark houses. Near the Havel Canal and Old Love. The tavern's fat owner sleeping too, lulled by the canal's tiny waves. And her son, caressing a woman. Perhaps.

> *For those who are born to write fiction and poetry, it is never enough to be in love, because a work of art needs intellectual fiber, which love lacks.*[4]

All memories are dead. Now you, too, are a memory. You, too, are dead. I have no choice but to return to the words I've kept inside me, carried with me, lived and breathed. How did I ever endure this sky without my words. How did I endure that avenue, that night, those nights when I lay sleepless in bed, my thoughts racing—unable, when I got up, to translate those thoughts into words. When at night, in the depths of a deadly sleep, I confronted existence and found it so very small. This life that sates me only when I have taken the lonely wind that blows inside me, the love that loves inside me, the death that dies inside me, and my very will to live, and turned them into words.

Nothing else.

You are a memory now. Made of flesh you can take anywhere. I shall never, ever chase after love. I do not find love convincing. It's born of thoughts and molded by thoughts. The more you think about it, the more it grows, and deepens. The more space it commands. The more it occupies your thoughts. Never to come true. Only to become more abstract. Endlessly abstract. Like life. Like death.

So long as one is spared the pain of separation, love can be endured, while to suffer true loneliness is to waste away in a dungeon.

From the moment two bodies intertwine, love ceases. Even at that timeless moment, the moment of orgasm, isn't each lover alone, doesn't love still long for more. At the moment of birth. The moment of death. Love can always move to a new object of desire. To other moments, persons, cities, streets, and hills. However deep your thoughts, your love will match them. That's how ravenous it is. And agonizing. The agony of life.

I feel no longing. I expect nothing. I feel no pain either. I'm not hungry. Not sleepy. Only this fog of anguish settling over me. All around me. My street. My room. My pictures. My memories. My childhood. My child. My blood. Myself. Ah, but it's so much greater, and deeper, where I go in search of emotions. Where I brush against the soft skin of long nights. The nights when the sunlight finally finds us. Or the bare tree in the backyard. Now you want to become a dead memory.

You seek it in other cities. Crossing other borders. You want to go even farther. To the city of my past. The city where I suffered. The first big city I saw as a child. The city that made me miss our little town in the countryside, from the moment I set eyes on it. When we arrived at a house that was no more than a shanty. To stay with my father's relations. The day we arrived. One of their children had died the night before. The child was lying, waiting, in one of the dark rooms, under a white sheet. His mother was crying in the next room while we children played in the hall. I kept hoping for the door to swing open so that I could see the little child's body. Mixed in with my longing, a great fear. On the rainy day when I saw death for the first time, in a house where I was staying for the first time. The body of a nine-year-old child. You want to go to the great city, to the house where my books are lined up on dusty shelves along a narrow corridor. The city as dusk descends, as my hills reveal their contours and my trees cast long shadows that I inspect one by one, I tell myself: "This is where you'll die. You can go where you wish, but you must return to these hills to die. To find your own death."

This was the city that acquainted us with the world. We rode the trams. Got lost in our first crowds. Then we came to understand how different each person was from every other. We entered youth. Went to cafés and taverns. Watched the artists. At night we went to the same bars as they did. Some of those artists are dead now, others have moved to faraway lands. We first came to love men's bodies in this city, or we tried to. We got married, we got divorced. There were nights when we could mock the whole world. Some of us sank into depression. Some of us died of cancer. We lived through politics. With forbidden poems. With a handful of human rights. But it all grew inside us. It grew. Sometimes our love for humankind outstripped our loneliness, and sometimes, some people brought us a kind of loneliness deeper and more agonizing than solitude. Then we'd go to watch the city's seas. Watch their waves cresting, to remind us of eternity. Watch the north wind ruffle their blue-green surfaces. No one was happy in that city, but no one was sad either. Because no one could believe in happiness. You're in that city. Leaving me with winter and songs of death.

Now I have rediscovered my childhood expectations, across from these houses and avenues . . .

Walking these avenues, passing these houses, I find the answers to my childhood questions. The child inside me is talking. My life is here. A life that knows no limits. A child's picture circumscribing it. But here, now, it's infinite. At least for those who can reach that far. So here it is. In the shape of this row of houses . . . in the shape of this avenue. In the shape of this bare tree. In the shape of an old woman. In the shape of a drunk. Immersed in your childhood longings, you carry on . . . An image of a city, divided by a wall—as a child I saw no such thing. There were no images, either, of lonely old women. Ready for death to take them at any moment. These images are new. Beneath a department store, a dark restaurant. Old couples sitting at tables, eating chocolate cake. Reliving the lost moments of their lost pasts. They are no longer alive. Nothing more to do in life but eat chocolate cake and wait for death. I want to do everything that this earth offers, except to be an old and lonely woman in Berlin. Enduring Berlin nights. In Berlin's old buildings. I need to get to the cemetery long before that can happen. A lonely corpse can stay alone. But never a living one. As a child I could grasp the meaning of infinity, but not the loneliness of an old woman.

I did not know that to grow up was to grow old. That to see Mora was to see death.

Do you not know why you came into this world? You must write it, only write it, forever hungry, forever thirsty . . . your end must be a horror and a misery! How can you not know? Pavese told you all this.

I cannot recall a thing. Not a single tall building. Or their aspect, or how wide the avenues are, or how extraordinarily high the buildings. Not the weather or the particularities of the language. Not the clothes people wear, or what they're like, how they behave. The only ones I can recognize in this city are the Turks. And little by little, its dimensions return to me. I shall will this city back to life. Does the green dome just opposite belong to a church. I don't care if it belongs to a church, or a library, or a theater. All I want to know is how the city in its entirety has affected me. I want to know what in this city still speaks to me, after an absence of twenty-one years. The city park appears before me. The warm summer evening I spent there, the young man I was kissing. Images of

JOURNEY TO THE EDGE OF LIFE

the walk home, through twilight or the sun's early light, after long nights spent seeking new experiences, learning about the world. Through one courtyard and then another, to reach the house. Each courtyard has a great wooden door with a great iron key. To get to know people. To know human love, carnal love. No, no. I'm no longer gripped by that young woman's terrifying quest. I no longer search for new experience or human warmth. Today, what love and human warmth I feel, I carry inside me. In other words, I am loveless. And cold. I carry images of the city with me. All my travels, all my human portraits from my life of travels. Or from the places where I settled. Looking back, but no longer to cherish those living or departed. All are now joined in an all-embracing love for humankind. And there I stop. In the generality of emotion. Nothing else. A love abstract and universal, as capricious as a summer cloud. Prone to sudden downpours. No match for a light breeze. I am the downpour. I am the breeze. And when the sun comes out again, to warm a cloudless sky, I shall be free of the cities and railroad tracks and nights and mornings that have, like my loneliness, brought me both misery and happiness. Nothing inside me but the emptiness of having no room for more. I shall be alone. And independent. Like a tree on a lonely plain. Large and very old. And alone. In that valley. On that hill. I am proud of my wayward ways. I am all that's left of all the images I've carried with me, of sleepless nights and sunrays, of walks and trains and buses and ships and planes, more than I could ever count. All the hours and days and weeks and months and decades I've spent looking, looking at bodies, books, gallery walls, museum corridors and their vast exhibits, and in Istanbul, the surface of the Bosphorus. All my conversations with people I knew and those I knew not at all. All those loves that were already ending from the moment they began. All the bodies I have loved. All I have left of the world's countries, its systems and governments and bureaucracies, its democracies and police forces and football teams and wars—all I have left now is the emptiness of knowing I have room for no more. My independence. My wayward ways. Fixed as any tree standing alone on any plain on this earth. I have no wish to go back. Not for a year, not for a single moment. To think of all those closed borders I'd have to breach once more, to reach this boundless space. I no longer have it in me to fight for human rights, not here, or in any other country. By country, I mean both the land of my birth and the earth in its entirety.

I am here, in this city.

Sitting in a café where two great avenues meet. I seem to remember that green-domed building just across from me. But I don't want to know what it is.

Three tall buildings to the left, two to the right. I'll order another rum. The clock across the street says 13:31. Two arrows below, pointing to Pressburg, Budapest, the airport. Behind them a wall announcing itself as the Burg Theater, building number three. On the square that seems deeper and longer every time I look, two statues. The first is a man on horseback. I have no desire to know what emperor or hero it commemorates. Beyond

JOURNEY TO THE EDGE OF LIFE

it is a monument to some military victory. This one made of steel. A man holding a flag, trying to climb up high. Farther back, beyond the line of rooftops, a modern high-rise. The telecommunications tower, perhaps. A tower with or without a restaurant. Twenty-six hours ago, I sat beside Kafka's grave. In that empty, green, and silent Jewish cemetery, beneath a tree. Beside a grave. Now a one-armed man passes by. And all at once, another image from twenty-one years ago. So many crippled men back then. One leg. No arms. No hands. Some of them must be dead by now. Survivors of the war. But some are still in life, and one of them is making his way across the avenue. This is live war footage. This is as far as I'll go. I don't want to answer any questions about where I'm from. I come from nowhere. Other than myself. It's Saturday, we're sitting on the chairs that the Italian restaurant on Carmerstrasse has set out on the pavement. It's muggy. Cloudy. Rain is coming soon. I'm dead to the world when suddenly I wake up. At once it's clear. You'll be awake all night. You are not the sort of person who defines yourself by the work you do, the trips you take, the people you know, the cafés you favor, the friends you seek, or the things you like to do. To the contrary, you are simply yourself, whatever you do, and that's why you can never decide when to travel. For wherever you go, you are yourself. Two hours later, you're on a huge plane bound for Frankfurt. From there the plane will continue to London and San Francisco. What a storm it takes you through. Tossing you up and down. In Frankfurt you put the child on

30

a flight to Stockholm. This child sets such faith in the real world. It breaks your heart. You don't even want to think about that northern country. Or the people in that country who are dear to you. No place for emotion. Or time. What a beautiful thing, to think that there are people who can set aside all thought of life and death, the better to devote themselves to the serious questions of the real world.

> *—There's no room for people like you. You bring me pain.*
> *There looks to be a storm brewing in her head. Her eyes*
>   *are blood-red.*
> *Stefano smiled:*
> *—We came into this world to make ourselves suffer.*[5]

You board a bus. Heading for the city. The only other passenger is American. And the driver is a foreigner. Just three foreigners on this enormous bus. A lifeless Sunday in Hamburg. The wind the only living thing. The driver is playing a cassette. Random music, designed to evoke emotion. And with it, perhaps, longing. Nothing else. But it stirs up pain.

That is how you live through the fourth of July. You buy a train ticket and then you walk around the station's front entrance, or its side walls, or its back entrance. You remember walking around the great harbor when you visited this city some months ago, and the escalators that took you down beneath the river, and the bars, the red-light district, its old prostitutes and its young ones. You've come now to a pedestrian precinct. The dimensions of that great harbor on that cool summer evening. And here it is, another cool summer day. A day that makes you think of autumn. Lining these avenues, buildings, shops, department stores, and the occasional restaurant. Shops selling the same things as in every other city or town. All closed. The square is lined with stalls. Stalls selling the same third-world goods as every other town and pedestrian precinct.

A cool wind.

Sausages on the grill.

Fathers watching their children.

Mothers trying to relax.

Beyond this pedestrian precinct, the avenues are empty. The restaurants too.

Like I said. A living breeze. And Sunday.

A Sunday as dead as the Sundays I spent in a petty bourgeois neighborhood in my own city thirty years ago. Except that these houses have an elegance. The stores, too. Everyone is nicely dressed. But there is no breath in them. None at all.

I'm sitting in the restaurant car of the train taking me from Frankfurt to Berlin's Zoo Station. A man sitting across from me. Soon we start to speak. He tells me he's a lawyer working in Berlin, but he lives near Hamburg. Quite a few rich people have left Berlin for political reasons. They come here from time to time to do business, but they prefer their houses and gardens to be in the West, where they find it safer. Now he's extolling the blessings of Catholicism. I love listening to people. I'm genuinely interested. To know what they think and how they look at life. But wherever I travel, I rarely meet a truly independent person, a person who is free of medieval thought.

Catholics are the most difficult people on earth. It would be better to converse with a stone. With water or a cloudy sky, or even the silence of the night. But not with a university-educated Catholic. Is this lawyer telling me he voted for the Christian Democratic Union. But he doesn't think much of Kohl. He says the party needs a more forceful leader. This lawyer has two good qualities: the first is that he chain-smokes, and the second is that he likes a drink. Even better, he smokes Camels. You can tell from the smoke. Another thing in his favor: he's friends with every single person who works on this West German train. He even defends them, on matters of little consequence. And of course they all talk about the war. Of course they do so on a train where you have only to look out the window for a clear view of its consequences.

Now a horse and carriage passes before me, carrying tourists. They want to live in seventeenth-century Vienna. In the middle of all these exhaust fumes, this traffic. The sun is getting warmer. For the first time in four weeks, you can go to a café and sit outside.

There is a life to live.
Bicycles to ride.
Pavements to walk and sunsets to savor.

You leave the hotel. It's your legs walking, not you. You're not in Vienna. You're nowhere. There's nowhere you want to go. You let your legs decide. You try not to look at anything. You see that you're passing the Turkish Consulate, and all at once, all is clear. Your whole life comes rushing back. But you push your thoughts away. Stripped as you are now of purpose, direction, nationality, emotion, and temporality, these associations cannot reach you. You've been sitting in this café for three hours now, summoning memories from twenty-one years ago. Your only wish to gather up the details, and only the details, of the last three days.

The McDonald's across the street. One of the city's more recent arrivals, most certainly, these American chains have spread right across Western Europe.

It was as a direct result of Hitler's fascism, I say, that Germany was divided and the Berlin Wall built.

"It's good that Germany was divided," he says. "Otherwise, its industrial output would have caused a Third World War."

"We gassed six million people," he says. "We shouldn't have killed them. But we did."

He says this as casually as if he were ordering another bottle of beer. This scares me. It scares me, and it shames me as a human being. I wake up in the middle of the night and remember how calmly he pronounced those words. And suddenly I am wide awake.

It's Monday, the fifth of July. Four o'clock, still night. Or rather, already morning. The sun has risen. Maybe it's been there all along, beyond the clouds and the rain that have greeted me every morning for a month now, perhaps there was, at this hour, the North's never sinking sun. Four hours later, I'm walking the streets. More rain clouds now, in the sky above these gray buildings. The rain stops and starts. I get wet, I dry off. The city is empty. No one here except the old women being forced to wait for their final journey. Some of them board the 19 or 29 bus at half past nine precisely to go to the West's greatest department stores. To marvel at the lacework and the handbags, the wristwatches, bridal fabrics and summer fashions, and every other kind of merchandise imaginable or unimaginable. Just to kill another day.

The avenues in this city are long. Some of them too long to walk. They go on for kilometers before leading into a square or an interchange from which other avenues radiate. Impossible to know which one is the continuation of the avenue you've been walking on. Storkwinkel is a small tree-lined street inside a triangle of main roads along which traffic flows day and night. There are only a few buildings. Old buildings on one side of the street, new ones on the other. There's a man walking in front of you. You watch how he walks, notice how it strikes you. No one in this city walks with such indecision. When you go to open your big heavy old door, you see him waiting there, still hesitant.

—Have we met, he says.

—No, you reply.

—My friend lives on the second floor, he says.

You know of a girl who lives there, alone. A fleeting memory now, of a day, a day when night had come early, an ambulance parked in front of the house, police entering the building, and later someone coming out on a stretcher, face covered. The concierge telling me that this girl had been hospitalized after a suicide attempt.

—Is she here?

—She escaped from the hospital and came to me. She didn't want to go back.

We climb the stairs together. She's desperate for someone to talk to. She needs to be with people. To share her despair.

You are staying in a large, bright, empty room that looks out to the treetops and the sky. For all its commotion, this city is painfully still.

—I brought her here last night. She hasn't slept for days. Drinking beer and smoking. Drinking beer and chasing sleep and waiting to die. Would you like to see her?

You know you can't do a thing for this girl. But together you go downstairs. The rooms down here are rented individually. In each there is a sink. A large room for communal use. The people living in the other rooms never knock on this woman's door. She's in bed. Holding a beer can. Smoking. One or two dying plants, a few old books on the shelves. Quite a few books by Hermann Hesse, you notice. Too many beer cans to count.

She's so thin her skin is hanging off her legs. Her eyes, dim with fear and deep with despair. She has lost the will to live. From time to time she cries out. Though she must be in her thirties, she looks forty years older. On the brink of death. We go back upstairs.

—We were lovers, her friend says. But then she gave up on everything.

—Alcohol won't help her, I say. She needs a good drug to get her to sleep.

But I cannot bring myself to think where those drugs might lead.

I call emergency services. Her friend talks to them. It goes on for so long . . . It's as if they've both forgotten about the girl downstairs, the better to console each other. And also. This person he's speaking to is neither a doctor nor a psychiatrist. Maybe it's a woman who does nothing but answer the phone, maybe she's lonely and needs company. Maybe it's an hour later when he puts down the phone, and I ask:

—What did she say?

—That perhaps those wishing to get better should get themselves to mental hospitals of their own accord, and leave those who don't wish to get better to curl up and die where they are, he says . . . he says.

And suddenly you remember madness. You see a girl on a summer's day on the Aegean shore, in a vegetable garden, leaning on a fence, drawing water from a well.

On the radio they're reading out the names of fugitives wanted by the authorities. You are overcome yet again by the agony of that pull to eternity. You think about the long and difficult path between madness and independence. How strong you needed to be. The time it took, the pain you had to endure. You want to send this man back to his friend, return to your beautiful independence.

There's a boy sitting with his parents at the next table. They're all looking at me as if it's a crime to sit at a café table and write. I'm in Vienna now, on the Kärntner Ring.

On my way to Zoo Station to buy a ticket, I see the girl again. She's going into the supermarket just ahead to buy more beer. This city cares nothing for its wretched alcoholics or its infirm, or its old people, lost to dementia. In the station, I join the ticket queue.

A man is being beaten by four burly policemen. All the most desperate people in the city congregate at Zoo Station. Terminal alcoholics, their faces scarred, leaning against the walls, clutching their bottles and every so often cursing passersby. The man who's getting it from the police right now does not look dirty. He has even shaved. He's holding a half-finished bottle of whiskey. He tries to make off to the platform, the police knock him down. He shakes them off and heads for the platform again, and again they knock him down. One of the Germans in the ticket queue cries out.

—It's not just that man the police are abusing. They're abusing us all, he says.

This man has courage, I think. A man who can speak his mind. Shout it.

On my way home, I see the girl again, arm in arm with her friend.

—I'm taking her to the hospital, he says. Can't you come with me. Please?

—I'm about to leave for Prague, I say.

I have to get out of here. I can't bear the sight of all these old women; I can't bear to watch Turkish workers swarming into every store to buy the most useless things to take home with them from their summer holidays. Both things make me unbearably sad and hopeless.

Now I am at East Station.

Now the world will open up before me.

It will be for me to give shape to all that presents itself to me, everything that grows, breathes, wastes away, or is already dead—to knead all this into something greater. Whatever nature or dreams or feelings offer, I need to use all my senses to go deeper. Transform every object, every living creature, every human being, every fleeting image, make each one fully alive. I must make life larger, growing it in my own way, make it wider, deeper, send winds through it and pelt it with rain, until I can see myself as a single point, living or dead, born or unborn. Once I am sovereign of my own life, I must begin to grow my death. Until my life, my death—until they have together embraced every life, every love, every death.

You're in a train carriage made in Hungary. There he is again, sitting across from you. Maybe even the same height. Thin. Eyes neither blue nor brown. Green. After a while he shows you his paintings. Watercolors. Quiet scenes of nature. Expressions of his timid nature. Suddenly you want to give him everything. Your childhood, your fatigue, the eternity you seek in this journey. Your skin. Yourself. This man's skin won't tell you anything new. But neither will he remind you of anyone else. He won't stay a stranger. Or at least he'll stay as strange as everyone else. You will only have escaped the night. Escaped from yourself, your almost unbearable self. Only to find it in others: humanity, naked and strange. That's deep enough. Can you offer anything deeper. When do you think about all this. When he comes to lie with you in your compartment, on that narrow bed that no one could say was made of oak. When he lies there sleeping next to you all night, and you do not find it strange. When you think about abandoning life and this earth, and your mind refuses to accept it. Or was it the exhaustion of lying there all night, unable to sleep. He didn't sleep either. Whenever he found the strength to open his eyes, he sat up in bed to smoke a cigarette, while he watched you, while he stared into space. You won't see anything in Prague at five in the morning, he said. Except for workers heading joyously to work. We can explore the city together, he said.

You look down the corridor, to where you can see what lies ahead. Houses appearing, one by one. Roads. The morning is still cool, the sky will soon grow light. But there won't be an early sunrise. The clouds will rise first. It's cool in the train corridor. Huge crowds on their way to work in the twilight, as he said. I'm tired. We're already coming into the station. He's asleep. I write a few words on his cigarette pack and step down from the train. Leave my bag at the station and take a car into the city morning. It's not yet six, and I am outside the house where Kafka was born. On the wall before me, a metal sculpture showing Kafka's thin face. Suddenly I'm not at all tired. But you can hardly believe you are here, in front of Kafka's house, standing in front of this three-story stone house in the blue of an unexpected morning.

The years you spent with his stories in the stagnant cities of faraway countries so much more deeply ingrained in your thoughts and your very being than this moment can ever be. Or is every moment weighed down with the memories we carry with us. Is this Maiselgasse, Prague, or Tuna Street, Ankara. Or am I dreaming. Or have I fallen through time. Am I a traveler. A weary-eyed traveler sitting in a car, looking out at Kafka's house. What moment is this, in what journey. When I never go on journeys. At every moment and wherever I happen to be, have I not always been on the same journey as I am now. Is this not how I've lived my life. How I live it still. How I shall carry on living.

You're in the Ambassador Hotel. Old furniture, chandeliers hanging from the ceilings, sparkling white tablecloths, old waiters dressed in black in keeping with tradition. Have you gone beyond seeing the world through the eyes of the Stoker.

Now an Anatolian woman crosses the Kärntner Ring, wearing the clothes she wore in the fields.

By the time you reach Hradschin, the sun is high in the city. The houses on Alchimistengasse are hardly two meters high. He worked at number 22 for nearly a year, writing his stories. The house is closed today. Tomorrow you'll be gone.

A while later you walk down to the river, crossing over to wander the streets until you reach the old Jewish cemetery. At first you take it for a modest cemetery hidden in the folds of the city. Large gray and brown tombstones, roughly cut and crowded together in uneven rows. Tossed together as carelessly as if they've been thrown away. Whatever shape they once had now lost. Bending every which way. Curling into each other. Surrounded by the backs of gray buildings. Houses long abandoned to the elements. Like the houses back in Galata. Some of the windows are broken. Surely there are people living in them. The dark silence of their interiors seeping through their open windows. This must always have been a place of shadows, you think. And the air in the cemetery is more humid than the air in the city outside. The air of the cobbled streets. You walk deeper into the cemetery, and it opens up, opens up, expands, grows and grows, drawing you into its infinity. Deeper still, it is a cemetery so full of life as to hold you there forever. You leave. An old guard is sitting on a small wooden stool next to the gate. In the small wooden hut opposite, he sells the city maps and brochures that no tourist can be without.

—Where is Kafka's grave?

—Not here, he says. The newest graves here date back to the seventeenth century.

—Yes, I say. I saw. I even saw some that date all the way back to the fourteenth century.

—Take the metro. To Želivského. That's where you'll find the Jewish cemetery where Kafka's grave is.

You walk from street to street. You hear animated voices. You pass under arches. Through a doorway, into a wall of sound. A dark beer hall where everyone is knocking back one beer after another. Still in their work clothes, waving their huge mugs, swigging down the beer so fast you'd think there was a competition. How you envy people who can drink all day and still work. The world is so much easier to bear when you're good and drunk.

You continue on your way, dragging your feet now. When you get to the metro station, you see that you don't have the right change. The girl at the turnstile signals for you to pass through. Money has no value in this city. The escalator takes you deep into the earth. At the last stop, you travel back up with everyone else, up to the light of day. You cross the street. The cemetery gate is open. Just inside, an arrow shows you where you need to go. Dr. Franz Kafka.

Never has the end of life seemed more distant. Until this moment, I've seen the end of life in every face, every breath, every growing child or aging woman, every embrace and morning. Even as a child, in the wheat fields, in the summer moonlight, in the darkest depths of night, I saw the end of life, but when I moved away from all that, when I began to travel on foot or by train through towns and villages and fields and vast landscapes, past mountain ranges and along the shores of lakes, rivers, and endless gray seas, watching people I knew nothing about recede into the distance, my every image of them more distant, until they vanished altogether—only then did I move away from the end of life.

Why does the wild green silence of this place make you forget the world in which you have been forced to live. Have you found peace here beside his grave knowing it was here in this world that Kafka suffered such pain. As if you have nowhere else to go. First his father and then his mother, buried in the same grave. In Vienna now, you think about Kafka's letter to his father. The father who bore down on him all his life is now lying on top of him in his grave. How strange that this didn't occur to you when you visited that grave yesterday. Perhaps you took some comfort in seeing that he was not alone. Your thoughts then were with Milena and his sisters, who all died in the Nazi camps. It brought you great joy to think that Kafka had not lived to see those camps. Tuberculosis might have claimed his life too soon, but it had saved him from that horror.

Death will come and take your eyes, death that watches over us by morning and by night, deaf to the world, disguised as a dreary errand, an age-old ache.[6]

As I leave the silence of the wild green cemetery, I remember my brother's words. An icy night in Berlin. The snow on the roads has frozen. On the side bridge outside Zoo Station, we're waiting for the 66 bus. He's on his way to Wannsee. To the lake on Berlin's western outskirts. To the large and silent house buried deep inside its garden.

—We have to find ourselves a burial plot in Istanbul, he says suddenly.

—I don't care where I'm buried. I don't even want to think about what happens to my body. Leave it to dissolve into the earth or into water, or ash, I say.

His words seemed needlessly sad to me that night. To be thinking of your grave on a cold night in Berlin . . .

In Prague now, as I begin my pilgrimage to the graves of the writers who have made me who I am, I think he was right. But I still don't want my grave to be in Istanbul.

He boards the bus. Sits beside the window. And I return to the Berlin night. To the cold and the dark.

You come to a park. Now you're feeling very tired. You lie down on a wooden bench. In the quiet. Some way away there are children playing. Their grandmothers or grandfathers watching them from their benches. People on their lunch hour pass you by. The people of Prague, you watch them all. No one else lying on a bench like you are. You're beyond tired. You cannot even walk. You cannot sleep. Cannot sit. That's why you're lying down. Through the fog of fatigue, you watch them watching you. This tired woman. As you do the same. You stare in amazement at this woman lying on this bench with a toothache and a sore throat, lost in time.

Later, much later, you regain some of your strength. You leave the park by the first gate you can find. At the bus stop you ask an old man for directions to the station. He asks where you've come from, and where you're going. He only knows the cities you mention from the war, he says.

I'm too tired now to do any more walking. I must lengthen these streets in my thoughts, live with them in my thoughts.

I'm at the station, waiting in a long line to pick up my bag. It has four wheels. I can roll it anywhere. And when I do, it makes a lot of noise. Everyone waiting to check in or collect their bags stares at this bag I pull behind me instead of carrying it. As if they've never seen a bag like this before.

I want to toss it into the middle of the station and sit down and cry. Scream. Scream about all the world's systems. Scream from the deepest part of me, where Kafka's words still live: "Wedding Preparations in the Country." "A Country Doctor." *The Trial. Amerika. The Castle, Letters to Felice. Letters to Milena.* From your diary. I'm ashamed to carry a bag like that. I'm ashamed of who I am. It is at that moment I decide to say as much as I can. To write. I have no choice but to shout and scream. So here I am, screaming. And again, I am the one who hears me.

You live by your thoughts. Others live by facts.

Walking up and down the platform, waiting for my train, I bump into Latislav. So it turns out I do know someone in this city. Someone whose skin I already know, for we've shared a night. He didn't go to Bratislava. He must have woken up as soon as I got off the train. Unbelievable. All day long, while I was walking the streets of the city, he was doing the same. It's not me he wants to see. This I know. What he wants to see is my independence, which carries within it my dependence on myself.

—I thought we were going to explore the city together.

—You were sleeping so well, Latislav.

—Have you seen Kafka's house?

The time I've spent waiting in stations, ports, and airports. Wanting to leave with every person leaving. Go on every journey. Even when I wasn't going anywhere, I was, from an early age, imagining myself on a journey that made life worth living, because it never ended. Before I learned how to do that, it had pained me, pained me so very deeply, not to leave.

Here I am again on the train tracks. Forests, small hills, cornfields—how familiar the countryside that passes me by as I travel for the first and perhaps the last time from Prague to Vienna. The color of the sky and of the ground, the shadows and the light breaking through the clouds, the darkness that will come later to engulf us, the passengers leaving and boarding the train at every station, the people in their villages and towns, the passing cyclists and pedestrians, they pull me out of my thoughts, my interior monologue, my love affair with myself, my mind's never-ending journey. It is only on a moving train that I can be myself, and at long last take in the real world. Everything that stands still bores me.

The boy was standing at the bare window, looking out at the cool, black hills, stunned by the scene before his eyes. Above the haze, all was still, all was clear. Beyond the leaves rustling in the dark, hills were taking shape. No sign of daytime's dead and colorless slopes or trees or vineyards or hills. No sign of life, only wind, only sky, only leaves, only nothing.[7]

My room is on the sixth floor of the Hotel Prinz Eugen, across the street from the side entrance to Vienna South Station. I turn on the radio. The one I longed for, the one who sat across from me on the train to Prague. He seems to be here to welcome me to this alien room in a hotel I'd never heard of. It comes from him, this aura of comfort, permanence, and contentment, and from desire itself, from this longing for love that we try to keep alive inside us, from the people we become through longing, and from the bonds our thoughts forge between us, even as we remain alone in our worlds. As we walk and smoke and watch and sleep and keep our silence. As we make love, and reach orgasm. If we can hold on to this feeling, even depression carries meaning. Even if it does not take human shape. But from the moment it breaks through the skin, to flow on through the body, you can begin to believe in life. Then you want to live forever. You must never forget this feeling. Even if it doesn't take a human shape. This is the only feeling that defeats me, defeats the living creature inside me, and the dying one too.

On the sixth floor of the Hotel Prinz Eugen, the first thing I notice is how much furniture there is. Then I decide not to think about this anymore. I pick up the phone and dial a number. As always, he speaks very slowly.

—I'm in Vienna.

No reply.

—Call tomorrow evening, he says.

How he leaves me feeling. Soothed, relaxed, almost lethargic. This may be no more than my interpretation of his nature, of the way he smokes and watches and breathes and falls silent. Even his depression is comforting somehow. When he's absent. His stillness and his skin's timeless beauty: nothing in life, death, eternity, or this earth can match it. This is what draws me to the man, even when I'm not with him. Even if I'm constantly imagining myself with others. No relationship—be it with a person or an idea—can exist without a shape. This pliant stillness, this calming and consoling stillness, is perhaps the only emotion that still defeats me: both my living self and my dead one. His anger is perfectly still, and his disquiet. He draws life inside him, draws love inside him too. And when he makes love, in silence, wordlessly, transcending speech, evaporating concepts, erasing them, with each calm breath he feeds me with his strength, his silent distress and undelivered speeches, the unspoken phrases of his deep inner world, his unformed dreams, and the life he keeps concealed behind his cultivated calm, and in so doing he keeps me alive at the same time as he opens me to death.

I put down the phone. I'm under the shower. Under its hot and cold water, my drowsiness washes away, but not the journey without end or beginning still taking place deep inside me. All is good. Or would be if I didn't have a sore throat and a toothache. At some point in the middle of the night I awake to pain. I place an aspirin on my tooth and find a lozenge for my throat before falling back into a sleep too deep for pain to reach it.

When I wake up to a drip-drip-dripping, it's four in the morning. I get up. Close the shower door and the door leading out into the hallway.

Soon the city will come to life. Its workplaces will fill with working people. Its factories will change shifts.

Trains will arrive at stations. And depart. The planes in the sky will travel across it toward all the world's known airports. Ships will take in cars and cargo, passengers will board. Those who did not get a wink of sleep all night will rise from their beds exhausted. So too will those who slept for many long hours. Some will awake from nights that were happy, or painful, or full of love. Or anger. Some will ask themselves how they can get through another day. Some will contemplate suicide. Others with think of a city they miss. Or a person they miss. Some will die unexpectedly. Some will look out into a world where only the mountains and the fields do not look alien. Some will pray to God. Others will pick up a gun and kill someone. Or throw a bomb to kill people. Or wave banners with bombs painted on them. Some will be sentenced to death. Others will make short trips to distant countries to attend peace conferences. All the world's armies will embark on war exercises. Newspapers will be printed. Radio stations will begin their morning broadcasts. The fishermen of the Mediterranean have already pulled their nets from the waters. The women of the Mediterranean already have swept and washed their doorsteps. The trucks and the cars have taken to the roads. The bodies in refrigerated morgues lie waiting to be buried. Morning has come, to a timeless summer in a timeless world.

I spend much of that morning watching the city through the window. Did I have to acquaint myself with so many countries, so many people, so many novels and their heroes. Did I have to embrace their authors as my closest friends. Did I have to board so many planes, trains, and buses. Did I have to live through the nights of so many cities and wake up in the morning to walk their streets all day. Why have I never been able to confine my life to a small city with a single square and a handful of avenues.

Without another look at the city spread out before me, I sit down at the table.

II

I'm looking out at the wheat fields.

    I'm the only guest in a big new hotel. Sitting on a large terrace. After breakfast I go up to my room and lower the blinds. Darkening the room's whites and blues. I try to fall asleep. A strange sort of anguish overtakes me, in the half-light it grows and grows. An emotion from which I cannot free myself. Or is it a person. Now it's in the past, now in the future. Or is it the journey itself. This feeling I've been grappling with, all my life.

> *He was forced to keep all his fine feelings—all that he himself so wished to give up—locked up inside him.*

Isn't it always like that. When there is nothing we want more than to open our hearts, share the ebb and flow of our feelings with our lover, make ourselves fully known, don't we still keep it all locked up inside. Who answers to love. Love's most profound limits reside in its very beginning, and in its continuation. Only after separation does it open up to reveal its riches. I cannot defend the opposite of what I feel. I need distance, I need to find my feet again in the world of my own thoughts. I have never wanted to give all my love to a single person. My love knows no bounds, my wish to love all the people in the world. From time to time I've hated them all. Except myself.

Now I am flooded with emotions in need of careful examination. It's almost as if I'm stretching them, making them into roads that keep on stretching, kilometer after kilometer into infinity. But I need now to turn them into words.

When I woke up at three in the morning (now that I am for the first time in a room with a clock that works, I keep checking it) I told myself that—whatever else—I had those words. But what do other people do with their pain, their daily lives and sleepless nights, their hope and their despair.

I open the aluminum blinds and let the Yugoslavian sun flood into this blue-and-white room. This room they said I was the very first to occupy, when I arrived last night.

The sun warms the room. I'm just outside Niš. The only guest in this big new hotel. Others will be arriving toward evening.

I look out at the flowers bordering the terrace, at the E5 just beyond. In the evening, road-worn travelers will pile out of their cars. All knowing where they've come from and where they're going. They'll clean themselves up. Eat supper. Go to sleep. Too tired to think or read or write or make love.

I need to get away from myself. Slowly I make my way to the terrace. First I take a seat in the dappled shade. The waiter brings me coffee and mineral water. Then I move to a table right next to the geraniums. I want to be closer to the outside world, to the road. The sun slips in and out of the summer clouds. And now there is a cool breeze. Then the clouds clear and I can feel the sun on my skin. There can be nothing more powerful than the sun. It's even more powerful than I am. But I cannot begin to appreciate its power unless I first appreciate my own. And now here I am, sitting at this second table, just in front of the stairs leading down to this terrace. Writing.

I'm looking out at the wheat fields.

I shift my gaze, and my thoughts. Now I'm looking at the hotel. Now I turn back to the wheat fields. The wheat has been cut. Piled up now along the side of the road.

Not since childhood have I had the chance to look out over a wheat field. When I was small, when we went up to the high pastures in the summertime, I got to ride the wheat threshers. How I love those golden sheaves of wheat. Wheat fields were my seas in those days. My cities and my boulevards. My train tracks.

Now and again the waiter comes up to tell me something. Unless he is just speaking to himself. I'm not sure how much of what he says is for me.

A couple on the stairs to the terrace. The man holding the woman lightly around her waist. The terrace of this new hotel, where I sat in room 103 all morning, thinking.

Where I lay in bed all night awake. Tired beyond tired, after a journey of 1,041 kilometers. Trying to coax myself back into a more everyday sort of fatigue. Into stillness, and then into sleep. I've never had to wait for anything in life as much as I've had to wait for sleep, though there have also been times, times when life has become a random sea of pain and lost all its meaning, when I've buried myself in deep, exhausting slumber. Until I wake up, hopeless, drained of all desire, and still exhausted.

So here I am now, sitting under the Yugoslavian sky, on this terrace that runs alongside the asphalt road, which after skirting this wheat field will go all the way to Istanbul. Here I am, turning the feelings inside me into words, or at least making them visible. Trying to restore my natural connection to life and my own created world—to maintain the distance that keeps the outside world from damaging my own—to regain my old balanced pity for life. Still beyond fatigue's natural limits. I let myself relax. For a moment, I let myself lean back. I close my eyes. To bask in the heat. A gust of wind sends my papers flying. I chase after them. Pick them all up. Pick up my pen again. There in front of me, between the wheat fields and the E5, weary workers on their way back to Turkey from Germany. They're trying to rest. They will not succeed. They will never be able to rest.

Not even in death. These are people whose deaths have been taken away from them, just as their lives have been. They are castaways, with nothing to call their own but their wages, their cars, their department store tat, their bruised and battered inner worlds. That night, as I lay in sleepless exhaustion, the first guest ever to occupy room 103 of this new hotel, I imagined someone sleeping soundly, and so happily, in the empty bed next to mine.

Or was it he, sleeping beside me. Didn't we come to this hotel together. No, I'm alone. My only companion the toothache that has made itself so fully felt for the past five days. After days and days of headaches. Headaches are a constant. I'm used to them. But how is a person to bear a toothache when in the last four days she has flown from Berlin to Hamburg, returned by train the same day to Berlin, and then, on four hours' sleep, gone to East Station to board a train for Prague, and spent that whole night lying next to him, on the edge of sleep, watching him smoke, and then, after walking the streets of Prague all the next day, boarded an evening train for Vienna, arriving that same night, and after that it was Zagreb, Belgrade, Niš.

You did have a good night's sleep in Vienna, but it was not enough to put things right. You left the hotel and wandered around the city aimlessly. You sat in a café for six hours. In the afternoon, the late afternoon, he finally arrived.

—I almost didn't recognize you, I said.

Now you're looking out over the wheat fields on the other side of the E5. A group of students is celebrating the harvest. They're standing in a circle, holding hands. Singing songs. Holding a red flag. You saw this red flag earlier in the morning. But you thought it was to warn off any Turks who might be tempted to park their cars there. You'd no idea it had anything to do with the government.

How it cheers you, this Yugoslavian morning that takes you back to those cool summer days in the high pastures. This day is so much better than it might have been.

We leave the café on the Kärntner Ring. We find ourselves on a wide avenue blocked off for pedestrians. I try not to notice how Vienna has changed. But I cannot shut my eyes to the grandeur of its buildings. Memories of these buildings come flooding in unbidden. The awe I felt for these splendid edifices on that, my first visit to my first European city. Feelings, feelings, feelings. Let go of these cities' splendid buildings, let go of poverty, let go of those roads, stations, passengers, foreigners, lovers, let go of your childhood and all the friends who've died in distant lands. Let them go, let them all go, and let yourself go with them, the self that is tearing you up inside. To other times. Or timeless times. GO.

Leaving Vienna in heavy traffic twenty-one hours after my arrival, I despair for the Black newspaper vendors I find at every crossroads. The destitute countries of their birth. The obstacles they've had to overcome, the problems that still plague them, the anger that Central Europe's happy but undeserved comforts must provoke in them, when they think back to the poverty that drove them here. The contradictions of their lives so tightly knotted that no matter what they choose—to stay or to leave—they can never be undone. The despair grows. The anger deepens. Ever restless, ever in pain.

The roadside clock says seven. The day is long, and not yet night. Not even close.

He wants me to find our street on the city map. I know nothing about maps. Nothing about this city either. Nor do I wish to know anything about this city. And anyway, my hotel will be easy to find. It's across the street from the side wall of South Station. Three days ago: Berlin–Hamburg–Berlin. Then: West Berlin–East Berlin–Prague–Vienna. Now, I am about to leave Vienna. Trying to erase all my impressions of this city from my mind. How can I be expected to find the street we are walking down on the city map. What avenue. What city.

These people have a single aim: to find freedom. To achieve independence by shaking off society's irrational chains.

Do you see this in yourself, have you ever felt like that. Lived independently or at least lived for yourself. Destroying nothing and causing no harm, never tiring, never giving up. Can there be any other way to reconcile yourself with life.

We're driving along this road for the fourth time. They're doing repairs. I pick up my bag from the hotel. We set off. The clock says it's seven. In this city where you spent twenty-one hours, you got some sleep. You had breakfast, drank one tea and six rums, and you're happy. You saw nothing of the city, it's as if you were not even here; as you leave, your mind is free of images. You didn't even talk to anyone. You just came and went.

We pass through villages and forests. The last light of the sun on the cornfields. You remember a story you translated many years ago. Pavese's "The Cornfield."

> *There's always a street that's always emptier than the others. From time to time I stop to look at an avenue like this. Because at that moment, having lost my bearings, it's as if I've never seen it. It is enough to feel the sun and the light breeze, to see that the colors painting the sky are different, and not know where I am.*[8]

On and on and on and on. Not a word shared. The daylight long gone. Darkness descended. We've crossed the border. Well into the night now. The farther we go, the greater my exhaustion. Stretching soon to a thousand years. On the outskirts of Zagreb, in a lot overlooked by tall buildings and packed with parked cars, we come to a stop.

—I'll sleep here, he says.

No chance I'll get any sleep in this place. Eighteen hours I've been wearing these clothes, eighteen hours I've been sitting. I need to take off these clothes. I could pull my eyes out of their sockets. Could tear out my hair, pull out my aching tooth, my stiff neck, my brain that is so tired of thinking.

I am way up high now. Alone, on the edge of a cliff. I can't bring myself down. I can't live. Can't die.

He drove for nine hours without stopping once. Journeying into himself all the way. Ever deeper, willing himself into the depths. Feeling the full weight of the anxieties that have made his life so intolerable for all his twenty years. (But why is it that I, at age forty, have yet to bring my own journey to its conclusion.) But please, don't end it. Don't end it. At twenty, he has a choice: to bow to society's irrational order or to exist. He doesn't want to fit in. He wants to exist. He leaves. He pushes at his limits. And so do I. I have yet to encounter anything that makes me want to fit in.

He's leaning back in his seat. His head thrown back. He's closed his eyes. Every window in these tall buildings is dark. The only light coming from the streetlights and the headlights of the cars on the E5.

Here on the terrace of the hotel beside the E5 where I am the only guest, I order some food. Between Sunday and today, I have traveled from Berlin to Hamburg and back again, from West to East Berlin to Prague, and from there to Vienna, Zagreb, and Belgrade. From the German Democratic Republic to Austria and on to the Yugoslavian republics. To reach this hotel near the Bulgarian border, I have pushed myself to the other side of exhaustion, and possessed as I am now by an intense vitality, I need to eat.

To tire myself out.

The waiter brings out a red tablecloth, over which he places another tablecloth, bright white, never used.

—I don't need a tablecloth, I say.

—Eh, this is a first-class hotel, he says.

Together we laugh about the hotel being first-class.

My watch is set for daylight savings time. But there is no daylight savings time in Yugoslavia.

It says 15:15. I put some food in my mouth but am unable to chew. If I close my eyes, maybe I can sleep. No, no, until I've put every word in my head into words, I'm not sleeping a wink.

I have to reach a moment like the one where he stopped the car, leaned back, and fell straight into a deep sleep. He, making his journey in a 1975 Opel. Me, the only guest in a first-class hotel on the E5, writing it all down with a cheap pen.

It is what it is, this world. Those who cannot save themselves cannot save anyone else.

Everything comes to an end. Even if it doesn't.

I look around me. What do I see. The usual black nights and gray mornings. The clear light of a familiar sun. It can astound with its beauty and shock with its light, but even when you are seeing light as if for the first time, even when you are awestruck by the colors that autumn life can give to autumn leaves, you can still hear Dr. Driver shouting inside you:

"How boring you all are!"

"How boring you all are!"

"You're all so boring!"

Sixteen years ago, while staying in a town in Anatolia, translating *Wild Strawberries*, I could not have imagined that there would come a humid August day when

I myself was in Sweden, picking wild strawberries with a painter and a photographer who had left Turkey many years earlier. It was like a dream, only more so. Those dark-red strawberries, from another world . . . Or are we picking wild strawberries in the promised land. Dear God, are we picking these strawberries in the promised land. Because within this silence, within this land where feet never touch the ground, where thoughts and words reach no one—within this chilly country where silence hovers between life and death, and its northernmost doors shield people too lonely to so much as lift their eyes in greeting, there might be many paths that lead to death. Here, then, does death stretch before you, immortal and eternal. Do not let your thoughts drift back again to summers past.

I turn my chair to face the sun. Now I am looking at green hills. All those months I spent in Berlin without seeing a single hill. Berlin is totally flat. No hills whatsoever. Whereas I'm a hill person. I'm carrying my images of Prague inside me. I think of Latislav. Latislav, who at twenty so wanted to push at his limits but did not stray beyond his country's borders.

Of all the restrictions in the world, none have troubled me more than borders, and within my own borders, I enjoy limitless freedom of movement. If nothing else, I can go wherever I wish, keep my own silences, and my own limitless screams.

My one day in Prague was richer in experience than most seasons. Now at last I can set down the words that have been gathering inside me for the past two days.

Until this moment, I had to keep my images hidden in the darkness deep inside me, unable to turn them into words. All I let them do was torture me.

Even my earliest childhood images. Ever since those cold nights of childhood. I've lived with them and loved them, and I've thought they loved me in return, but perhaps I've never loved or lived. I was only ever living and loving projections.

Saturday, July 20, 1982.

Morning. 5:15.

I've been up since four, waiting for my tooth to stop aching.

Last night, when all I wanted was to go to bed early and lose myself in deepest sleep—though the pain was so excruciating, and the aspirin on my tooth so bitter, and my fear so great that my toothache, growing worse, might wake me, I still managed to sleep for six hours. Now, though, the pain is so fierce that I can barely move the right side of my face. For the first time I think of my mother. Who lived inside her own silences. Who was like no other.

For the first time, I think of the child I sent to Stockholm from Hamburg Airport six days ago. And of what the child said:

—When people think while they're looking at things, it's really their eyes doing the thinking.

And not even nine years old.

I'm in the hotel room. The bed next to the window is empty. I could almost hear him breathing last night. In thirty-five minutes it will be twenty-four hours since

I heard a car moving away through the half-light of a Yugoslavian morning. He's on his way to my city. Maybe he's there already. Fast asleep, inside a house. Or at some other point along his 1,722-kilometer drive, and the journey into himself that has neither a beginning nor an end. Same as me. I am at some point along this journey of 1,041 kilometers that has landed me in this hotel. In that other city, only everyday life awaits me. There could be someone I love in the house I call my home, or someone who loves me. Or this love has worn thin after years of living together. We both want to live apart, we both know we're happier with others. But does the happiness we find in others stem from the life we shared. No, such relationships are false. False because corrupted by their surroundings. We should be as frank with each other as we are with ourselves. But this we cannot do. No, I cannot return to my old life in that city. It was all so random. If you give nothing to a day, the day gives nothing back. No chance there of walking down an empty street. Every street and every corner is packed with people, but for all its crowds, it's so very empty, empty, empty. The mystery of the city persists, and from time to time it makes itself heard . . .

But this, too, is an illusion. The city's mysteries are our memories' reflections.

However much I flitted from one thing to the next, I was stagnating. I do not wish to return to ordinary life. There's something inside me in need of release. I need to make sense of the life I've lived. Here on the road I shall hear my own cries, and only my own cries.

There is no such thing as fate, there are only limits. The worst writing comes of meeting those limits with patience. One must challenge them.

I open the shutters. I watch the overloaded cars of Turkish workers flowing along the E5. I've been watching them since Thursday morning. Those who know and adapt to their limits will never achieve the independence of thought that can only come from challenging those limits. Those who live within their limits and at the same time challenge them will spend their lives stuck in a cul-de-sac. Forever restless, doomed never to find contentment in life or to die with ease. The more they age, the greater their fear of death. They might succeed in putting on a show of strength for others, but they will know that they are lying to themselves. It is a step in the right direction, though, to know this. Some are so little able to think for themselves that they take lies for the truth. But we have a right to cherish our greatest gift, which is the right to life, just as we have the right to meet with eternity at its end. Life gives us such opportunities. They should not be squandered on the random comings and goings of the everyday. It is something to be molded and transformed and pushed beyond its limits. Not something, then. EVERYTHING. This is why I keep moving. To escape being pinned down. I'm not afraid to keep moving. To the next city or the next husband, or to turn in my tracks, to travel to another country, or a madhouse, only to leave again—none of it frightens me.

He parks in front of those tall buildings on the outskirts of Zagreb. The buildings' darkened windows, too many to count. The only light is from the streetlamps.

—I'm not driving anymore, he says.

—I'm leaving, I say.

I take my bag from the trunk and head toward the road. Toward an alien night. I stand beside the E5. I've lost all sense of direction. On these avenues going nowhere. Tall streetlights in front of me. Tall streetlights behind me. Above me, the sky and the night. Asphalt beneath my feet. Beneath the asphalt: earth. Europe, all around me. I need time. I need a place. I need just one familiar thing. I need to strip myself bare. I'm going nowhere. I head back to the car.

A journey can light up a whole day. But the nights kill me.[9]

No night has ever killed as much of me as that night in Zagreb. Not even the nights I've had to spend in the same room as another mental patient. Because mental hospitals can endow a person with a strange will to endure. Does this stem from our expectations, I wonder. Or from understanding that resistance is both pointless and useless. On the outside, though, there are no expectations, there is nothing to resist. The hospital of life or, perhaps, an eternal madhouse.

To think is to hold a conversation with yourself. To share with another person is to share with yourself. To make love with another is to make love with yourself.

To be with another is to be alone. Don't forget this. But Pavese is right.

It is what it is, this world. Those who cannot save themselves cannot save anyone else.

The most important task, then, is never to stop resisting loneliness.

   I'm back in the car again, sitting in the front seat. With my toothache and my sore throat. At a quarter to five in the morning, all the streetlights go off. The sky is growing lighter. Morning on its way. I get out of the car. Where do I want to go really. Where can I go. To want to go somewhere, be somewhere—isn't that the same as wanting to go nowhere. Is there anywhere left for me to be. I'm nowhere. I flag down a taxi. I go to the bus station. Now the streets are crowded. The buses are full, the queues for the next ones, too. The terminal is even more chaotic than Topkapı, and dirtier. Most of the passengers are villagers. Yugoslavia is a nation of villages. I get along well with villagers when I meet them in their villages. I feel uncomfortable around villagers who have brought their villages' customs with them to the city. And in villages that have been taken over by people from the city. Things going in the wrong direction in both instances. The buses are very old. Everything here makes me feel so hopeless. Filth, abandonment, and poverty. I am feeling dirtier, poorer, and more bereft than ever. Not a single image in my mind, tangible or abstract, with which to start the day. I am myself no longer an image. I'm dust. I'm a stone. I'm air that will soon be warming up. There is just one familiar image in this alien landscape. And that is the red car that carried us here from Vienna. I hail another taxi. But I can't speak to the driver. I point the way. Where to turn. Where the car is. Under which tall buildings. Which streetlights. Surrounded on all sides by tall buildings. By tall streetlights. Which parking lot. Every, any parking lot. The whole world is a parking lot. The whole world is a high-rise. Tall streetlights. No words I can share with this driver, no language.

Suddenly I say:

—Volvo.

On my way to the main road, I'd glimpsed a big Volvo sign behind the cars. But now again I'm on a long journey, searching for that one familiar image, that last remaining place of shelter. What if, after I left, he continued on his way. This possibility fills me with such hopelessness that I cannot help but laugh and bite my lips. There is the car, just where I left it. But now it's sitting in the sun. I pound on the window. He opens the door. I sit down in my seat. My tooth is hurting again. And again, I'm smoking.

At eight o'clock, he says:

—I'm ready to go now. Toward Belgrade.

—I am too, I say.

Though I should be going in the opposite direction. All day long, I'll be traveling farther and farther from my destination. What difference does that make.

The sun is shining.

For eight hours, he drives without stopping. On the road to Edirne, with thousands of cars carrying license plates from the German Federal Republic, Belgium, the Netherlands, Austria, and France. And I travel with them.

Each car packed with wan and weary passengers. The men at the wheel even more so. The women yawn. The children in a daze at the back. Stricken by a poverty I do not, cannot, share. Is it not a form of independence, to lose myself while seeking out my limits. One more day. For one more day, I shall be my own prisoner. Then I shall be myself, and at the same time, free of myself. Overloaded cars. Out-turned faces, swarthy and drawn. So many inhumanly exhausted people traveling onward, ever onward, toward their longed-for destinations, in these tin prisons they call cars. To be forced abroad to make a living, it's the great scourge of our age.

We are restless people who have to leave home to find peace.[10]

One of Pavese's heroes said this.
A Calabrian.
An Anatolian might say the same.

III

*He would, he thought, be traveling across the surface
of the sea to infinity.*

When people ask me what sort of work I do, or ask if I'm married, or what sort of work my husband does, or what my parents are, or how I myself live, I can see from their expressions how happy my answers make them. And I want to cry out to them. These answers you so approve of, they're superficial, they have no bearing on what happens underneath. Lacking as I do a steady job or proper place to live, I have no place in the "civilized" world. I do not see myself as a successful person. I might seem so to you. I am seen to be so because this is how you people see me. Without my ever lifting a finger. Perhaps without my even wanting it. It's so very easy, to stay where you place us . . . Whereas our inner lives, to which we apply our real talent and devote our hearts and souls, and our very existence—for you they have no value. You leave us to keep all this buried inside. But no—let me at least shout at you in silence. I care nothing for the way you order your lives or understand honor or privilege reason or measure success. I dress in such a way that allows me to walk amongst you. I dress well, too. Because you give the best seats to those who dress best. I am trying to walk amongst you. Because you've not given me permission to work as I wish. You've not given me permission to follow my own instincts. What I can do without effort seems to you an achievement. All my life you've tried to wear me down. In your houses. In your schools. In your workplaces. In your private and public institutions, you've been running me ragged. I wanted to die, and you revived me. I wanted to write, and you told me I'd go hungry. I tried to go hungry, and you gave me a serum. I lost my mind and you gave me electric shock treatment. I gathered around me people who could never be a family, but we still became a family. I live outside all this. All I know on this morning as I prepare to leave this hotel where I'm the only guest, with no idea where to go next— which train station, which port or airport—all I know is I am something other than a good, well-balanced, and successful person.

This could be any road. That it ends in Istanbul is just a coincidence. I didn't choose the city or the country or the roads, did I. I'm nowhere. I won't be anywhere. I shall adapt to nothing. In years to come, many thousands of travelers will come to stay at this hotel that looks so much like a space station. I'm just one of many. I'm here, watching the summer clouds wander past. I speak to people. I look out at the hills I've so missed. Isn't every hill my hill. Every patch of earth. Every person. Isn't every person really me. Don't we all carry all our love inside us. Why tie yourself down to a single person. The moment you shun conventional relationships, they push you to the margins. They try their best to cast you out. It's as if they don't even know how much society has alienated us all. I have rescued my mind from your clutches. It's over. From here on in, I shall stand on my own feet under my own sky. I shall walk toward the horizon's straight and ever-receding line.

I have never aspired to a beautiful relationship, or to any relationship of which the petty or haute bourgeoisie might approve. Never been dazzled by romance or been swept off my feet by a lover's wondrous and virtuous sincerity. Never settled down into a relationship that I hoped would grow richer with time. I've always seen such attachments as false. They are imposed on us by society. I'm against the institution of marriage. I always have been and always will be. If ever I've seemed to conform to your institutions, it's because I have come to understand that this is my only way to resist them. The only way for me to resist success is for me to match your success. I have no wish to think otherwise. My aim in this life is to change how people relate to each other. I know of no moment more miserable and hopeless than the moments when it seems as if change will never come.

Change will come. Just as all else on the earth's sphere will change—its mountains, oceans, lakes, plains, steppes, deserts, riverbeds, glaciers, towns, and villages—so, too, will human relations. A time will come when we are no longer forced to live in contravention of our instincts. A life of conformity is stagnation and nothing else. Nothing else. So there I was yesterday, sitting on the terrace of the new hotel. Warmed by the ravenous sun. Tracking the ravenous rays of light. I thought about a November sky. The clouds hanging above a forest. Dense clouds, marbled with shadows, black and white and every shade in between, bringing winter closer. Here and there, peeking out from their deepest folds, tiny patches of blue. The paths of light streaming through those gaps to travel westward with the wind.

Yesterday I had company at my table. A truck driver. The hotel engineer. The men who are putting in the pool. We had coffee and cognac together. One of them had just left his wife and was feeling very bitter. Love comes, love goes, we said. We drank to separations. All separations, all love. How friendly they were, these people with whom I shared a few never-to-be-repeated moments of a July evening.

We're back on the terrace as the sun prepares to rise over the hills. Once again, we're drinking coffee and cognac. One of the men is called Zoran. He tells me it means sunrise.

Now it's eight in the morning. I'm taking a break from writing. I need to get going. I need to see new images. I need to keep going until I've found an image

I can embrace, an image that will bring calm to the turmoil inside me. I'm heading to Santo Stefano Belbo now. It's as if he's waiting there for me, this writer who's been dead for thirty-two years. To see his hills, his houses, his streets, and the patch of nature that made him who he was—won't that be a bit like living him.

I'm not getting back on the E5. I need to take other roads. Every road I travel needs to be a new one.

It's cloudy. On the E5, a steady stream of workers heading back to Turkey. I can't understand it. Nothing around me makes any sense.

Though none of this is unfamiliar. It's just impossible to understand or accept. The only values we can accept are our own. And they are so very different from those imposed on us. And it's so very hard, to live in opposition to the social order. It's not at all easy, it's not even possible. There is just one thing I do not find strange. And that is my own existence. It is, perhaps, my only source of happiness. My only connection. From this I know that I must make sense of myself, or my life will have been wasted.

The only sin is to fail to understand one's own deeds.

Everywhere I go, I'm surrounded by people going on vacations or returning from them. Arabs, Germans, Yugoslavians, Turkish workers, people from all over the world. A large bus stops in front of the hotel. Packed with Turkish workers. Working people lack pretension. Tourists are unbearable, wherever they happen to be.

I need to retreat behind my walls. I'm not suited to

life under the sky. I can only look at the sky from behind walls. As in Genoa, the sea will elude me. As it is for me, it is for everyone like me, we all live behind our own walls. Our streets and our trees, our loves and our sandy beaches, they live in our thoughts. Our thoughts their only limit. Our whole world.

Leaving the hotel to stand at the roadside, I am assailed by a nihilism I have not felt with such force since adolescence. The scene before me an exact replica of the picture I had then of the world.

It's drizzling.

The harvested wheat stacked in bales on the field. The young people have left. The young people who'd been dancing with their flag. I don't like flags. I've never liked them, even as a child. Yesterday's warm sun has vanished. Zoran did not arrive.

The bus has come from Istanbul. Fat women stepping down. Wearing long, colorful skirts. Carrying large bottles of water. They eat a lot and drink a great deal of water, these people.

How I long for Santo Stefano Belbo on that cloudy, drizzly July morning. To reach Turin. I've given up on the Mediterranean, on the seaside and the sun. Those places are for tourists. Whereas every day I've spent under this sky has been a holiday. Even the days I've spent working. Perhaps what I need to do, if I am to steer clear of humanity, is turn night into day, and day into night.

What is it that makes every aspect of life so difficult. Words. And having to be everything at the same time. Woman, man, child, and adult; sea, sun, night, and morning; fear and courage and infinity; limits, darkness, clouds. Loving and being loved. Moving. Standing still. Understanding and not understanding. The unborn and the born. Being and nothingness.

We are driving into the city. At the wheel, a man who works at the hotel.

This time the city is Niš.

We stop in front of a butane gas depot.

—This is what the car runs on, he says.

So we won't be stopping at a petrol station—even this thought brings relief. On the radio, they announce the day's temperature. I can barely understand a word. The rain still spitting down. Suddenly I am out of energy. My tooth still aching. Quite a few cars lined up outside the butane gas depot.

How lean these people are, and how silent. They don't look like they've been on holiday. But they do when they step outside again. A song I know is playing on the radio.

I've heard nothing about the World Cup today. This is my greatest happiness. Perhaps I'll have left the world by the time the next one comes around.

The next song is in English. American English, the world's new mother tongue.

Once in Niš, I go in search of a pharmacy. The city looks like every Istanbul suburb. Or is this actually Istanbul. The crowds around me could be crowds in any city in my country. The merchandise in the stores, the villagers shopping in the Saturday markets—this is village life come to the city, with the occasional girl catching everyone's attention with her fine clothes and good looks.

I buy painkillers and antibiotics. I'm back on the street, dragging my bag behind me.

Why am I here. So far away from everyone. In a city, a country, where I don't know a soul. I'm tired. If I wasn't tired, it would be even worse. But why am I here. Is it to string words together, is it to push at my limits, is it to travel until I'm so tired that I fall into bed in the first hotel I find. Why were you so determined to lose yourself in a city you didn't know . . . but this is not so easy. Aren't you tired of these winds. Ask yourself . . . haven't you had enough of these clouds. Screamed your fill.

These women in black headscarves remind you of the ones in Istanbul, the ones we saw as exceptions, even before they actually were.

I go into the Ambassador Hotel. Inside are more tired Turkish workers, on the way to Turkey or on their way back. As tired as eternity, every last one.

I leave at once.

I remember staying here for just one night many years ago, on another journey, this during my years of greatest pessimism. The return of an old memory, musty, dreadful, terrifying. How much stronger I am today, how much happier to be alone. Even with this terrible toothache. As I search. As I take myself to the edge, as I travel to the end of what is possible, how I savor my independence with every new moment. How I treasure my solitude. How very happy I feel.

All the flights are full. I'm sitting across from an old woman in a café. Swallowing my pills. This toothache is my strange constitution making itself known. Giving me the pain I need so as to forget all my feelings. But enough is enough. I remember nothing now. I miss nothing. Want nothing.

No seats for me today on any flights to Rome or Milan. I go through the whole list: Istanbul–New York–Chicago. The Sydney flight that lands in Istanbul. Yugoslavia–China, Yugoslavia–Kuwait. Yugoslavia–Britain, Yugoslavia–France. Yugoslavia–Scandinavia. Yugoslavia–Netherlands. Yugoslavia–Belgium. Yugoslavia–Federal Germany. Yugoslavia–Austria (Vienna). Yugoslavia–Italy. Yugoslavia–Spain. Yugoslavia–Turkey–Egypt–Syria. Yugoslavia–Libya–Malta–Tunisia. Yugoslavia–Algeria. Yugoslavia–Iraq–USSR–Poland. Hungary–German Democratic Republic–Bulgaria–Czechoslovakia–Albania–Romania. The domestic routes: all full.

I buy a train ticket to Venice.

Now I'm sitting on the second floor of a high-rise in the city center. Which country is more chaotic, this one or Turkey. They're one and the same. Before me, a victory monument. This country's victory is another's defeat. Both built on human corpses.

The air in this restaurant, thick with smoke. Filthy tulle curtains. Ash-filled ashtrays. Impossible to breathe. In every mouth a cigarette. All that's missing are the street vendors. The nouveau riche with their gold teeth and their gold chains around their necks, their silk shirts and their big cars. What a relief, not to have to see them for a while longer.

A child is shouting. I'm leaving for the station. This atmosphere is unbearable. As I pay the bill, the waiter asks:

—Where are you from.

—Nowhere, I say.

He asks if I'm following the World Cup.

—Not at all, I say.

As I head down the stairs, I hear someone shouting.

—She's German. German.

On the bus to the train station, I rest my eyes on the women sitting across from me, and though all in this world is foreign to me and I lack the wherewithal to read their eloquent expressions, my thoughts still reach them of their own accord. I am no longer seeking words to match my feelings as I ride to the station. I feel better having left the E5 and that new hotel. Because now I am nowhere again. I'm not sad. Nor am I happy. I have traveled far from bitterness.

If all one had at one's disposal was a balanced mind, life would be unbearably boring. What beauty exists beneath these skies more resembles an assembly of lunatics.

The loudspeakers at Niš Station announce the trains arriving from Istanbul or departing. All services end in Istanbul or start there. Here I am, trying to get away from Istanbul, and everywhere I go, it sends reminders.

On mornings like this, all of life becomes a game under the sun.

JOURNEY TO THE EDGE OF LIFE

I'm at Niš Station, walking past one long carriage and then another. Here, too, there are people stepping over the tracks to reach their platforms.

One train has some cars coming from Munich and Paris, and others coming from Vienna South Station. The one on the other side of the platform began in Sirkeci and has cars going to Munich, Paris, and Vienna South Station, and this is the one I'll be boarding. What if I didn't, though. As I walk between these two long, dark trains, the thoughts and memories and longings that I have been pushing out of my mind come pouring back in with the rain the clouds have been holding back all day. Do I not see tired workers staring down at me from the dark windows on each side.

Movement. Yes, it's good to be surrounded by movement yet again. I'm not leaving. I'm on the rails, crossing cornfields.

But I—but I am far from all cornfields and all empty skies.

All the distance I covered on Thursday. Now I'm doubling back.

Thursday. July 10.

I think back to Thursday. The hours I spent drifting between sleep and exhaustion, unable to close my eyes. The moments when I did my best to embrace that exhaustion, as heavy as death. While listening to Mozart's clarinet concertos, hour after hour after hour. Deadly exhaustion, to the tune of Mozart, mile after mile. At this journey's end, I would meet Zoran. I did not travel

1,041 kilometers just to meet him. Or to forget someone, or to be with someone. The only reason I traveled 1,041 kilometers was to push myself forward.

I want to explode. Come apart. Go to pieces. I am sharing this compartment with a father and two children. A girl and a boy. The girl is older. Both children are clutching identical straw hats. This tells me that their father is taking them to the seaside. Suddenly I remember my own childhood. The old, slow trains we'd take to the cities and shores of the Aegean. The father who'd take us to Bozdağlar and Gölcük. Without straw hats. I loved trains when I was a child.

But buses upset my stomach and made me vomit. Once, years and years ago, decades ago, when we were on a bus skirting Bozdağlar to make the descent to Gölcük, I saw the bright-white body of a drowned man. Why am I remembering this on a train bound for Trieste. What is it about these children who are on their way to the seaside with their father, clutching their hats—why have they brought back that horrific and long-forgotten image. Do these children feel the same fear and curiosity as I did when they look out at the mountains and cornfields, nature and the sea.

But I—but I am far from all cornfields and all empty skies.

This is a direct train from Niš to Belgrade. I'm already looking forward to exploring Turin, to wandering its streets. But first I want the winds of Trieste to brush against my skin. The winds of Svevo's city. Svevo, who though he loved Ada with passion consigned her to misery in *Zeno's Conscience*. Literature's deep waters, churning with love and contradiction, pain, tears, and suicides. I trust them. I trust in literature, my true home.

Now, as I move between the hills that are soon to surrender to dusk and the night sky, I let go of my selves, both real and imagined. I am lost, I am forgotten.

I've taken the pills for my terrible toothache. I'm numb. The pain seems to subside, only to return with a vengeance. And screaming is not an option in this train compartment. And so it continues, all the way to Trieste:

Me, exhausted and nursing a toothache.

All else forgotten.

Journeys are so interesting. They cut away from the flow of life to take their own shape. To take you past mountains and coasts, cities and their nights. Past people. They show you rivers, they show you crowds, they take you in and out of stations, some empty, some full. Somewhere along the way, they take you through a forest. A forest that you might have already passed through several days before. Or a city. Did I pay any attention to these trees last time, you ask yourself. The ones with russet leaves, or green leaves, or no leaves at all. A child is standing at the roadside. Holding a big black umbrella. Wearing a green woolen cap. In one hand, a neon-green plastic bag. Next to him, the two sheep he's tending. He cannot see the lonely void engulfing him. He cannot see beyond it to imagine other worlds. The worlds we all build around us. The roads stretching out ahead. To new worlds and new lives, as all journeys do.

Suddenly he realized that the night opening before him was the sky. And all his eyes could tell him was that when dawn arrived he would be sitting on a train, moving through land baked by the summer sun. He saw that he would be free to come and go, and that he would forever be shut away inside his invisible human walls. These were his limits. His prison, silent and lost to the void. To the night.

IV

I'm in Trieste, sitting on the balcony of my hotel room. Looking out at three huge rooves. Television antennae. Chimneys. Summer clouds in the sky. Sunlight piercing through them.

It's Sunday.

A quarter to ten.

When I stand up, I can see pale-yellow buildings rising up on either side of the narrow street. When I step back from the balcony, the rooftops seem more compact. In the distance, more rooftops, shimmering in the hazy sunlight, blocking my view of the city. Beyond them are all the countries I've visited, all the countries I've come from. All stretching out before me. Calling me to infinity, along the line of the world's views.

In this city, Sunday does not trouble me at all.

The balcony walls rise as high as my shoulders. It

comforts me, it makes me happy, to see nothing but this balcony, these walls and the rooftops opposite.

Soon you will go out and walk the city streets. The streets you came to know in Svevo's writings, the streets you've walked in your thoughts and dreams. Reading him for the first time, beset on all sides by Istanbul's unbearable chaos, how you envied his heroes as they walked the boulevards of Trieste. All around you, there were bombs going off. No day, no night, without gunfire. With every new moment, another death. The only escape from the hell that was Istanbul was in books. And now, to walk those streets. Walking the streets of a city is one of life's great gifts. In your own city, even if there are no bombs going off, there's nowhere left to walk. Every street and sidewalk, every shop window, and even the sky and the air and the surface of the sea—as far as the eye can see there are cars, there are dark and billowing crowds. Is there any city more foreign to you than your own. The city whose depths you hold so dear but cannot bear for a single moment. The city you are slowly abandoning. The city that refuses to present itself to you as a single image until you move away.

Now you have come to Trieste, to walk its streets. For the first time in months, you are by the sea, the sea that is the same sea as the one you already know. In a matter of hours, the morning cool will give way to the summer heat.

These winds, with their whiff of seaweed, you know them well. Outside the hotel, a medieval square ringed by cafés and galleries awaits. I'll go out there this evening.

JOURNEY TO THE EDGE OF LIFE

A boy is sleeping in my bed. Tall, slim, and handsome. Bodies that are always present but fade when they are near, receding with the first caress. Vanishing bodies, longings lost. Lest I hem myself in with inanimate objects—walls, beds, armchairs, televisions, radios, paintings, glasses, faucets, sinks, bathtubs, curtains, balconies, chairs, skies, chimneys, rooves, porches, longings, memories, songs, or expectations—there is someone lying in bed and breathing. His sleeping form brings life to the blue bed and the navy drapes, the silk velvet armchair, the little television, the bar, the hall, the bland painting on the wall, the blue-black bathroom. This small balcony, this round table, these gray and white metal chairs—all are endowed with his vitality and youthful beauty.

It's my own younger self I see sleeping in that bed. The younger self I shall be dragging behind me until the day I die. Wasn't I both old and childish when I was young. So now here I am, sitting on this balcony in the morning haze. While behind those navy drapes, he lies sleeping, as the day grows ever warmer.

Last night he took me in his arms. Placed my head on his shoulder. Last night. When the train stopped at Belgrade. And I had reached my limit, passed over the edge.

Now, as thin lines of sweat roll down my legs, I am treasuring the beauty of a forgotten feeling. The church bells ring every hour. From time to time, I hear someone speaking. A steady stream of cars and mopeds. But none of these noises can dent the silence of Sunday.

When the train pulled into the station in Belgrade—when the corridors were packed with Yugoslavs and

Northern Europeans on vacation—when the two children traveling to the seaside with their father were eating their supper, watching the world through childish eyes and still clutching their straw hats—while their fathers talked nonstop with four friends who had gathered at the compartment door—while these hearty, fat-fingered men passed around their white wine, and gobbled down slabs of bread and salami—and later, when they unbuttoned their shirts and fell asleep next to me, snoring as their big, taut bellies rose and fell—when the train stopped at the Belgrade station and my toothache went off the charts, even though I had taken three painkillers and two doses of antibiotics since boarding the train in Niš, I took another one of each.

And suddenly I was engulfed by fever. Every part of me was in pain. Nothing left to me except my painkillers, my deadening exhaustion, my antibiotics, and the distance I had covered in my six-day journey from Berlin to Hamburg, Prague, Vienna, Zagreb, Belgrade, Niš, and now Belgrade again. My temperature rising fast now. It felt as if my heart was about to stop.

—Do you need any help? asked the Greek sitting across from me. What are these pills you keep taking.

There I sit, haggard and exhausted and in unspeakable pain, and sitting across from me, this Greek. In a white T-shirt and yellow trousers. Very young, very thin. Hair cut like John Travolta's. He's been reading German writers in Greek translation, writers like Mitscherlich and Dieter Lattmann who have nothing to offer a foreigner. Later on, I'll discover that he's never heard of the great Greek poet Ritsos. He's immersed in his young world. Knows little of the world beyond it. Little of his own world, even. More elegant than he perhaps deserves to be. That's all I've seen. But when he asks me if I need any help, I can't answer. I can't speak. I just point to my aching tooth.

He's going to Turin, too. To see the Rolling Stones. He couldn't bear to miss out. He plays the guitar and he loves the Rolling Stones. He's traveling all the way from Thessaloniki to Turin to see them.

All night long, I rest my head on his shoulder. I do not faint, nor does my restless heart stop. I rest my tired, heavy, aching head on the shoulder of a twenty-year-old man. He gives me back my youth, so that I can endure this night. He carries me into the heat, where I can sweat again. He returns me to the life I shall take with me to Piazza Unità d'Italia and Svevo's streets this evening. This man I have only just met. This young man, who doesn't know a thing about me, shows me more affection than any of the men I've ever held close. I won't go on to Turin tomorrow. First, to embrace this city's winds. At ten minutes to five, an orchestra starts playing in the square. A light tune to set the mood for the evening, rising up from the square to usher us into the beauties of the night, and life's embrace.

Together we leave our hotel for the piazza. A little stroll. A short segment of that longer walk into infinity. The roads on which we walk disappear into green hills. Returning to the shore, we are met with gentle raindrops. Harbors always remind me of the ones in my own city. But this harbor is so still. Nothing moves. None of the sea's joyous tumult. For a moment I think back to Istanbul rising above the shadows of Sarayburnu. I think of the ferry station at Haydarpaşa, when Christa was still alive. When she and Achim and Süm and I waited for many hours one day for the ferry out to the islands. I remember riding through that island's empty streets in a horse and carriage. The silent anticipation of its houses and gardens. Christa is cold. We're all cold.

Sitting in a café on the square, I feel strangely at home. Even the rain has stopped. Around us are people of all ages. No one looks lonely. These are people who live under the sun. They stroll across the square, young and old, bronzed by the sun and fashionably dressed. From time to time, a thin woman in black weaves her way through the crowd. An old man walks into the café, wearing white linen, brown-and-white shoes, and a straw hat. Reminding me of what my father liked to wear in Gölcük. Then I remember my brother putting on his brown-and-white shoes before leaving to meet his friends in Taksim.

The pigeons I thought I'd left behind in Istanbul, they're here too.

The Greek is silent, as am I.

—When did you visit Thessaloniki, he says.

—What year were you born, I say.

—1962, he says.

—That was probably when I was there, I spent one night, I say.

I don't mind what he thinks of me. I never worry about that, not with anyone. Maybe I'm selfish, but wherever I am, it's my own responses to people and their surroundings that interest me. At least that's what I think I deserve. I gave myself this right, just as—from a very young age—I gave myself the right to sleep with anyone I wished. I am disinclined to deny anyone what is life's most precious gift: our desire to be with others, skin to skin.

—What a nice woman you are, he says.

How consoling it is on this warm summer evening to look into this sea of unfamiliar faces and see one I know.

The bells are ringing. It's a quarter to seven.

Before we leave the hotel, as I'm combing my hair, I look at the wan face in the mirror and see a child in Gerede, dressed in her school smock, black with a white school collar, her hair tied back with taffeta ribbons. I see a pupil who recites heroic poems on holidays, and a young housewife who rushes from city to city, seeking other worlds. I see a woman who is loved and abused by two husbands, a woman who loves and abuses two husbands, a woman who is deceived by two husbands and deceives them both. I see a woman who learned how to resist, drawing only on her own resources. A person whom life has never cast out. You turned the end of life into its beginning, I say . . . If you attempted suicide at age eighteen, it was because you intended for your beautiful young body to frighten those who found it—take my body, you wanted to say. Take this cruel life. They cured you. The life they wanted for you was crueler still. So now you, too, are cruel.

Then you pushed against the limits of reason. Because they were suffocating. Impossible to spend an entire life within their confines. Another dimension was called for, though it was not in everyone's grasp. A way of being that went beyond reason, into something deeper.

The dimensions of madness. Since earliest childhood, I've been exploring this other realm, making it my own. Courageously. Never holding back. This has been my single greatest achievement in life: going where no one else has dared. Because they lack the courage. Because they dare not step beyond the limits of reason. But I—I have traveled into madness and explored its depths. That thin line between reason and madness. As thin as the horizon where this hazy Mediterranean joins the sky. Where the sea ends, and the sky begins. Let no one scold me for being selfish. Every self is selfish. Every patch of ground is earth.

Every life, and every part of life—it is what it is. The pigeons are taking flight. The café orchestra is playing romantic tunes. Melodies that call back old longings, lost longings. Soldiers parade around the Piazza Unità d'Italia bearing flags. The church bells ring. Seven o'clock. Now the orchestra is playing "Bésame Mucho."

—Do you know this song, he asks.

—Yes, I do, I say.

There he sits, in all his youth and elegant beauty. Silent but so very alive. What am I to do with him. There is nothing I want from anyone. As the summer crowds swirl around us, some walking their dogs, others deep in conversation as they step in and out of the cafés, he strokes my arm. As children play ball or ride bicycles, as pigeons rise into the sky, he strokes my left leg. Why don't I suggest a stroll.

A few steps, and we're by the sea. The sun sitting opposite the misty hills. These must be Svevo's hills, Zeno Cosini's hills. The hills where Ada's husband, Guido, took his long walks. The hills where jealous Zeno played with the idea of pushing Guido to his death.

We pass through the silence of the Sunday streets. The wooden shutters of the old buildings lining the roads leading up into the hills: all closed. At last, some hills to climb. It's been months since I climbed a hill. I, a child of the Bosphorus hills. A tomcat mating with a female on the top of a Fiat. On the ground floor of one building, an open window. A man in the kitchen. A transistor radio on the shelf. The scent of herbs, taking me back to the Princes' Islands. The sun is sinking behind the dark-green wall of sturdy pines. We're now at the top of the Castello e Cattedrale di S. Giusto. I write this down in my notebook. Ever since leaving Istanbul, I've been carrying around this notebook. I find a sentence by Svevo: "Perhaps it is my destiny, never to settle down."

The bells are ringing again. Eight o'clock. The sun is still sinking behind the pines. Through their branches I watch the sea turn orange, then red. Creating the world anew. How rich is each and every moment in this world. If you know how to see.

Later, after we've climbed back down to the Corso d'Italia. Sunshine still playing on the walls of the old buildings. Soon these streets will be in shadow, and the sky will grow dark, night will fall, leaving the lonely to their loneliness, the ailing to their infirmities.

The streets are empty now. From all directions comes a mechanical sound that always takes me back to films set in Mussolini's Italy. A very beautiful young girl sitting on a motorcycle, watching a football match. The sound of the same broadcast coming out of every open window, and from time to time, a chorus of shouts.

—Who's playing, I ask the Greek.
—Italy, he says.
—Who against, I ask.
—The German Federation, he says.
—Is this the final, I ask.
—It's the final, he says.

Which means that everyone in this city loves football. Because the Greek and I seem to be the only ones still outside. The only ones walking into this beautiful evening's fading light. Here and there, a man standing on a deserted boulevard, or sitting on the terrace of a shuttered café. Like monuments to loneliness. Detached from time and the world, never rejoicing in life, never joining in, ever captives of their solitude and isolation. A cat is sitting in one of the shop windows. Along another narrow street, through a pair of half-open shutters, I see an old woman smoking. A tired woman's aging face.

In the restaurant there's just one table without a view of the television screen. It's empty. The people around us are all testaments to summer and sun and life and health.

JOURNEY TO THE EDGE OF LIFE

But their eyes are all on the football, and their thoughts. Floating above the aroma of eggplant, cheese, and pasta. The summer heat. There's still daylight in the streets outside. The long days of summer, insatiable summer. A pause in the match. A lively Rolling Stones number. I stand up and ask one of the television viewers about the concert in Turin.

—Tomorrow, at eight p.m., he says.

I go back to the table. The best thing about the Greek is his total lack of interest in football.

—The concert is tomorrow at eight, I say.

—What train should I take tomorrow, he says.

—The 6:45, I say. But why not go tonight. Seeing as you slept all day.

There's a train leaving for Turin in an hour. At 22:08.

These curtains and walls, this warm and slowly falling summer night, these hills rising above the city—I must now take them in alone. As we turn into the Piazza Unità d'Italia, the whole town roars. As loud as an exploding bomb. Italy has scored a goal.

The room's been cleaned. The Greek picks up his suitcase. Again we are on the shore, heading for the station. He, carrying his suitcase. Around us, all is darkness. The scent of phosphorus rising from the water. Such a gentle night. Cleansed of all pain. Exhaustion erased, and with it, all thought. An evening you wish you could caress. And on this evening you wish you could caress, you stand by the sea and bid farewell to this man about whom you know nothing. You send him back to the station from which you brought him. I feel light, I feel weightless. Like a summer wind. On the Aegean, all summer winds are gentle.

Returning to the room, I turn on all the lights. Turn on the television, too. There's a film playing. I try to identify at least one of the actors. No luck. I take a mineral water from the minibar. At last I manage to turn on the radio. The Rolling Stones. It looks as if Italy's won the World Cup. The joy I feel now that my toothache is beginning to abate. All I ache for now is a long, deep sleep. Nothing else.

The announcer announces:

—The Rolling Stones!

It looks as if everyone in the city has come out into the streets to celebrate the victory. Good that I got back to my room and locked my door just in time. How glad I am to be alone.

Now all the cars in the city are honking their horns. Over and over, without a break. I try to open the window, but what a ruckus, such shouting . . . So it looks like another night without sleep. After nights of being kept awake by this toothache, which is finally abating, now, with all this commotion, I can see I have yet more sleepless hours ahead.

I go downstairs. The same man behind the desk.

—Did you win, I say.

Beaming, and without saying a word, he raises up an Italian flag. I go out into the square. The entire city converging. The many streets leading into this square, all clogged with cars. No one can move forward or backward. On every surface, in every hand, and wrapped around every back: an Italian flag. Every last woman, wearing a flag as a shawl. Even the children. They're all dancing, shouting.

—Viva l'Italia.

Even the children who aren't old enough to speak.

Italia, they all shout. Half-naked girls sitting on cars waving flags, symbols of victory. Others jumping into the fountains, screaming with joy. I go back into the hotel. The only person who does not appear elated at this victory is the elderly hotel cleaner.

—Mamma mia, he mutters, as he empties the ashtrays in the television room. Looking oh-so-grim.

I didn't want to hear a thing about the World Cup, but then it exploded over my head. And now I can't even think.

—Unless there is a cloudburst, they'll be shouting all night, says the old cleaner.

—I'm so desperate for silence and a long sleep, I say.

—They'll be celebrating again tomorrow, and for days on end, he says. Shall I bring you a cognac?

—I'm on medication, I can't drink, I say.

—Then let me find you some earplugs, he says.

He has to be the smartest man in the city, this cleaner.

Smart and sound of mind, and so healthy for his age. In spite of all this commotion. In spite of his job.

V

I wake up to sunlight streaming in from the edges of the navy drapes. It's 6:20. I meet with the same fatigue that sent me to sleep. At once I turn on the radio: *Don Giovanni*. I read for about two hours. I take a hot shower and then a cold one. The Italian World Cup victory is the first item on the news, and as far as I can ascertain, the President of Italy will be greeting the team on its return. I try to go back to sleep. It's not happening.

Since leaving Berlin I've heard nothing about the Falklands crisis or the Israeli war on Palestine.

Fate, which kills people, calls on us to remember the dead and hold their bodies in our gaze. Fear, everyday fear, offers no escape. It is shaming to see the truth: the reality staring back at us. Every corpse could be you or me or us. There is no difference. If we are alive, we owe it to the defiled corpse of another. This is why every war is a civil war. Every martyr is like you and me and calls on us to account for his death.[11]

I'm slowly packing up my things. It's Monday, twelfth of July. A muggy day. My toothache isn't so bad today, but I have a terrible headache.

Now I'm in the city library, in the Italo Svevo section. His piano sits at the entrance. On the wall above is his portrait, in oil. Painted when he was advanced in years. By the same artist friend who was so jealous of the young girl he loved in *As a Man Grows Older*. Now I have before me all the writer's photographs.

So much passion in the eyes of that young man. He lost his hair when he was still very young. Here is the young man in *As a Man Grows Older* (who felt old even when he was young). A very bushy mustache, which in his youth is turned up at the ends. Even then, he had an old man's countenance, as he would for the rest of his life. A photograph of his wedding day. The greatest chronicler of marriage in world literature, on the day he took his vows. His anger about love and the meaningless contingencies of marriage everywhere evident.

A photograph, signed by his wife: "A mon Ettore, Livia." December 20, 1895. A woman who loves her husband. A photograph dated the thirtieth of June, 1910, shows her with her extraordinarily beautiful daughter. At 17:30 I shall be meeting this daughter, who is now eighty-four years of age.

Another one from 1895. Svevo's wife is very fat. The

next photograph shows her dressed in white lace, holding a white silk parasol, and her daughter dressed in a sailor suit with a white collar and white sleeves. Svevo, standing between them, eternally restless.

In yet another photograph, he is standing in front of a bookcase. The same bookcase I can see before me, with his initials engraved in the glass: *ES* (Ettore Schmitz).

A handwritten page from a chapter of his Zeno Cosini novel: "The Story of My Marriage." A photograph of him arm in arm with his friend Veruda, at a time when the streets of Trieste were still full of horses and carriages. All the people I brought to life in my imagination while reading Svevo's books: they are here, in these pictures. Svevo: world literature's most dedicated smoker, who went through at least sixty cigarettes a day. Who needed cigarettes to stay balanced. Who wrote so very beautifully about love, death, and jealousy. Whose genius was to bring to life in his pages the emotions we manage to keep hidden inside us, except when we are reading him.

I think back to my days in Istanbul's mental hospitals, when I, too, smoked sixty cigarettes a day. There was nothing else I could do. They tried to take away my freedom of movement. They never succeeded. And today, on the twelfth of July, I am sitting in the Svevo section of the city library, reveling in the scent of four hundred thousand books. Could I ever want more independence than this.

I understand better now why I have traveled these 1,041 kilometers. With every departure, with every journey, I go deeper into the unknown, closer to self-understanding.

I'm very curious about Svevo's daughter. His only child. He was forced to marry her mother after falling in love with her sisters and being rejected by them both. According to the librarian, everyone in the city adores her. How eager I am to meet this woman who now lives with her adopted son and his wife and daughter, having lost her own three sons in the Second World War.

Leaving the hotel this morning, I went to a bar where I drank my tea standing up. They'd hung a white sheet on the wall behind the bar and painted an Italian flag on it. I read the words below: "Italy–Argentina 2–1. Italy–Brazil 3–2. Italy–Poland 2–0. STAY CALM: Italy–Germany 3–1."

The stores are shut today, as is the custom in Italy on a Monday. Gigantic headlines in every newspaper: WORLD CHAMPIONS! 3–1! HEROIC!

Half an hour now before I meet Svevo's daughter. Who will open the door. How will I pass from room to room. I shall ask right away if I can see photographs of her aunts. She speaks both English and German, I'm told. As was common in the haute bourgeoisie at the turn of the century, she was educated by private tutors. This will be my first ever visit to a house of the haute bourgeoisie. The haute bourgeoisie that time left behind.

I've come straight from the library. Via Principe di Montfort 12. A great blue-gray mansion. Too many windows to count. All of them shut against the world. Even during the day, not a single shutter open.

The mansion has two entrances.

Cars parked outside the café in the little square. From time to time, someone passing through it. Even this square is a world unto itself. A world of stones, cars, asphalt, pedestrians, card players, flags, cafés, and Celentano. But for once in my life I shall travel as far as Santo Stefano Belbo.

The old men are singing along with Celentano. I remind myself never to let go of the insatiable desire for life that has sent me on this journey. This is how I wish to live.

I do not wish to leave one part of me on Prague's Golden Lane, and another at the station. Or consign one emotion to Hotel Nais in Niš and another to Trieste. I need to take them all with me, feel them stirring inside me, to the very end of life. I do not wish to walk down through the vineyards of Santo Stefano Belbo with all my emotions spent. I need to stay restless.

Reading the poster on the café door, I see that the circus known throughout the world as the Italian Circus is known in Italy as the American Circus. Twenty-two minutes now until I knock on Letizia's door. Leaving behind me this world of football and circuses. What bliss.

It isn't me I see reflected in the images I've brought with me on this journey. It is Prague. It is the people in Prague Main Station who stared at my suitcase. It is the countless queues and loves and passions and aches and consolations and deaths and suicides, it is the boundless realm of literature that has set me on this road, through words and beyond them. And now my quest has brought me to the door of Montfort 12.

From Via Montfort 12 I went straight to the café on the Piazza Unità d'Italia. It was twenty minutes past seven when I left.

Throughout my life it has been from the dead I've drawn my courage. The dead in whose stories I have lived. The dead who succeeded in turning this world of damnation into one where it became possible to live. The dead who in their writings gave us everything in this world we could ever need.

They only have dwellings of this size in Italy. This country is now the mother of the world in my eyes. I walked up a flight of marble stairs. A young girl was there to greet me. It was only on my way out that I gained some sense of that great marble hall into which she ushered me.

She opens a door. I walk into a room. A room that would only count as small in a palace. The window to the left looks out over a green and silent garden. I sit down on a three-seat sofa. I look around me, but there are so many paintings and antiques to choose from that I don't know where to rest my eyes. I search for a portrait of Ada. A very beautiful woman walks in. At once we embrace. I've known this woman since she was in her mother's womb. She is wearing a black-and-white silk dress. And a jacket made of the same material. Black stockings. In one hand, a walking stick. In the other, a black handbag.

—Old age strikes some people in the mind, and others in the knees, she says.

And she gestures at her knees. These are her first words. Then, as she takes a handkerchief from her handbag:

—My dress has no pockets, that's why I brought my handbag, she says.

She has her gray hair in a bun. Her sun-kissed skin still vibrant. Her eyes are very green, very young.

—Shall we speak German or English, she says.

—German, I say.

I've never met a woman of this age so beautiful. In fact, I've never met a woman anything like her. I, who come from Anatolia. I can't take my eyes off her. The woman sitting across from me is more beautiful than all the portraits, chairs, chandeliers, art, and silver displayed in these stately interconnecting rooms. All that remains of her past is emotion, thought, and pain: literature.

I take in every detail: her tiny pearl earrings. Around her bronzed neck, a thin chain from which hangs a little cross. Antique rings on her fingers. On her wrist, an elegant watch.

Even her scent hearkens back to the turn of the century. It relaxes me, this scent, it banishes time.

—My father's grave is here, in the Giardino Pubblico. Right across from the James Joyce bust. I knew Joyce. He gave me English lessons. Not when he was living in Trieste before the First World War. In those days, it was Joyce's sister who was my English teacher. But during the war, in Zurich, he was my teacher. My aunts spent the war in Zurich, too.

—We all learned German, too. My father made mistakes when speaking German. And that was why my grandfather sent him and his two brothers to a Catholic boarding school in Germany. "A businessman must be able to speak flawless German." That's what my grandfather said. Whereas my father was interested in literature. Interested firstly in German writers: Goethe, Schiller, Schopenhauer.

It's still very muggy. Drizzling. But the sun still seeping through, as red as red can be.

Again the square is full of summer people, waiting for the festivities to begin. Another victory celebration, no doubt.

I have a mild headache. And my tooth is aching, just a little.

—My father started out working alongside my grandfather, in the Union Bank, while reading prodigiously in German, English, and French. He read all the Russians in German translation. But as I said, his first encounter with literature was through German writers. Afterward, he turned to the Russians.

(I think back to when I was thirteen and began reading Dostoyevsky and Gogol. Goethe and Schiller never spoke to me as powerfully as the Russians I read first. Then I fell in love with Hölderlin and Rilke. After that, I entered Kafka's boundless world. But it was the books by her father and Pavese that quenched my thirst and made my world whole.

—On returning to Trieste, he turned to Italian literature and found it entrancing. In the last years of his life, he also read Kafka.

—Not many of Kafka's books had been published at that time. My father spent a long time in London. My mother didn't join him right away. But later he bought a house and they lived there together. My father didn't know what to do with himself when she wasn't at his side. He felt lost: he was also a very jealous man.

(Could a man of such passions ever be otherwise.)

—My mother was thirteen years younger than my father. My father always said that no woman that young could ever love him.

(The same doubts that afflicted Zeno.)

—My mother fell ill after I was born. Her fever gave her convulsions. She couldn't have any more children. She went to Poland to recuperate. In the letters he wrote to her, my father kept asking if there were any young officers courting her.

There is, amongst the photographs, one that shows Letizia Svevo with her husband and her three sons.

—That is the last photograph of all of us together. We were vacationing at a ski resort. Two of my sons were officers at that time. They'd come back from the front. In the end, all three of them died. Pietro at twenty-three, Paolo at twenty-two, and Sergio at nineteen.

(The three grandsons with whom he once strolled through the streets of Trieste, all lost.)

Lost to the same war that sent Kafka's sisters and Milena to concentration camps and death.

Neither writer lived to know that pain.

—Kafka suffered so much during his life. My father was a man who hid his pain inside.

(Is it even possible to write, if not out of pain. When pain is too great to be held back from the border between life and death, when life can no longer sustain us—that is where literature begins, is it not.)

—My father never expressed his pain. He was ill before the accident that killed him. He smoked so very heavily.

(Zeno, chain-smoking.)

—Sixty cigarettes a day. He had lung disease. He couldn't breathe. After he broke his leg, breathing became almost impossible. He knew he was dying. He died like an old philosopher. He saw me crying, and he said: "Don't cry, Letizia. Don't cry. It's nothing. DEATH IS NOTHING."

Perhaps life is even more painful than I'd imagined. The café orchestra is again playing light music. Italy has the noisiest traffic in the world. The square is now even more crowded. The roar of conversation. In half an hour, it will have been a week since I left Berlin's Zoo Station.

"It must be my fate, to be forever restless."

—This is not the house my mother knew. Everything burned down. The house where she was born. The house she knew.

(Which means that the house where he fell in love with Ada at first sight has burned down, too. Of all those people I lived with and came to know, and whose hearts I tried to understand, of all the places I've known in my life, there is nowhere I've wanted to stay. I spend my whole life coming and going. No matter how far I go, I am always beset by a strange suspicion that I have never arrived.)

—Those houses were all bombed by the Americans in the Second World War.

—My husband had taken all my father's writings to our summer house, so we were able, at least, to save his books and his manuscripts. Otherwise we'd never have been able to publish them.

—It's true that he had a grand passion for that young girl. At the same time, he wanted to help her. She was a simple girl. All these courtships date back to the days before he met my mother.

(Svevo always loved young girls. Before her mother, and after.)

—The stories about his falling in love with my aunts are fantasies.

(But here, right before me. The portraits of all of Svevo's characters. How could it be a fantasy that he loved these aunts. Of course he loved them more, of course he wanted to marry one of them and not her mother. Perhaps Ada was his greatest love, great enough to make him forget all the others. Perhaps even she could not have done so. Because was it not by loving youth and loving life and keeping life alive and young that he freed himself from old ideas. Don't we all think of ourselves as both young and old, no matter how old or young we are. Doesn't every emotion carry its own meaning and its own unity.)

—A love like that was out of the question. My older aunt married a Bulgarian around that time. She had to leave Trieste. She later married a third husband. They lived first in Siberia, and then in Gorizia, and finally in Riga.

(So this must have been the great love story. So the story that ends in America in *Confessions of Zeno* actually ended in Riga.)

—Her husband died there.

(Guido, whom Zeno pushes to suicide.)

—It took him three days to die. He had a fungus growing under his beard, and that was what killed him. He couldn't see it, because it was under his beard. After the Russian Revolution, my aunt returned to Trieste with her two children. They're still alive, these two. Neither young nor old. One is over seventy.

—My mother died in 1961, at the age of eighty-three. She devoted her whole life to my father's books. The years after his death.

(I've never thought that a writer would be able to devote his whole life to his wife. These writers lived in the realm of the impossible. Where their wives' worlds ended, theirs opened up to infinity.)

—Since my husband died nine years ago, I've been very lonely. He was a highly educated man. I could speak to him about anything. His books, and my father's books in translation. *Confessions of Zeno* has just been translated into Japanese. Let me show you the book.

—Life with my father was a beautiful thing. Despite the dark thoughts he kept hidden inside.

(The dark thoughts that have chased me all my conscious life. What happiness I've known has grown from those dark thoughts. It is our dark thoughts that sustain us as we travel between life and death, love and loss, childhood and old age. Dark thoughts that never fade, never diminish, that grow in strength to become greater than us all.)

—He was always joking. Once, he said: "I stayed for three days in the country. For three days, I didn't smoke a single cigarette. I became a new man. And now that new man wants a cigarette to smoke."

—There were three pianos in our house. The finest of pianos. My mother and my aunts liked to sing.

(Again, I'm looking at the paintings. Zeno, trying to sing to please Ada. Only to make a fool of himself and lose Ada forever.)

—I used to sing, too. All the finest singers of Europe came here. Those days are gone now, alas.

(I cannot even imagine a house where the finest singers of Europe might come to give concerts. I'm most comfortable in houses I enter and leave, never to return.)

—After our three sons were killed, we adopted a child. But he fell ill and died. I've lost four children. My twenty-three-year-old niece lives here with us. She brings life to the house, she lifts our spirits.

(While it's always been for me to lift my spirits. There is precious little room in my internal world for other people, other lives.)

I am the only one working in this square. Apart from the orchestra musicians and the waiters. No one else is reading. Everyone is talking, laughing, taking in the crowds.

I should stop writing, at least for a moment. Maybe I should eat something. But I can't stop writing. I can't bear stopping all the time, just to eat.

I need to look at the calendar. It's Tuesday now. July. But what day in July. The thirteenth. It's two minutes to eight. I woke up at six again, just like yesterday. I'm so very tired. It took me four hours to get to sleep last night. I thought about Letizia's beauty. Of all the characters I've come to know in great novels, she is the only one I've met in real life. My chance came when she was in her last years, the last years of a long and painful life. Neither too early nor too late. I am haunted now by her beauty and humanity, her lyrical German and her poetic evocations of her past. She does not so much remember the past as carry it with her in the here and now. This is what makes her so beautiful in her old age. Letizia, who learned English from James Joyce.

Night is seeping into these great chambers that open up into each other. The streets outside are ceding to twilight. But in mansions like this there is twilight by day, and by night, broad daylight.

Letizia:

—Let me turn on the lights now so that you can see the paintings, she says.

I stand up. I turn on the wondrous lamps. And suddenly all is illuminated—the heavy furniture, the glass cases that look like shop windows, the paintings by Svevo's closest friend alongside paintings by Italy's greatest artists. Letizia's world as brought to life by Veruda, whom I know from her father's books. Strange as it may seem, these people look just as I imagined them when I first met them on the page. But I'm not sure I imagined

Letizia's clothes quite like this, or her hair. Such style this woman has.

—My father looked like his brother, she says.

She leads me into the next chamber.

—This is where I keep my husband's collection, she says.

—He collected first editions and manuscripts.

She hands me a fifteenth-century manuscript. Then she shows me his coin collection.

—My father never collected anything. He had one passion: cigarettes. He was very generous. He supported all artists.

We proceed to the third chamber. Here is a library containing all the translations of Svevo's works and all the books written about him. She shows me the diary Svevo's mother gave him. There is a poem on every page. Until his marriage day, he jotted down notes about the day beneath them. I see that one of the poems is by Eichendorff. Then my host shows me the book her father gave to a cousin. A dedication in his hand: "In memory of my cousin Livia, who fought so hard and so mercilessly to stop me smoking. And also, in memory of my having deceived her. A kiss given is a kiss never lost. Ettore."

—My father gave many books to my mother. Even Karl Marx. But that one she never read.

Then she shows me the book she wrote about her father.

—With this one, I won the Udine literary prize.

—My father had four sisters and three brothers. My grandmother had sixteen children in all. Eight of them lived. My father's youngest brother published a journal before my father published anything. He died very young, this uncle, and he was always urging my father to write, and telling him how good he was.

As we walk from room to room, Letizia extols her mother's beauty. I see her likeness in many oil paintings, all framed in gold. I see the book she wrote, and photographs of her at every age. But I keep wondering about Ada, I see no picture of her anywhere.

Letizia shows me her husband's paintings. She tells me he was the only man in her life.

—We fell in love at first sight. I was fifteen and he was seventeen. We met at a ball. Then the First World War broke out. He enlisted to fight against Austria. After the war we got married. Ours was a great love. We were lovers, and we were friends. In all spheres. All our lives.

(What is more important today—to love one man, or to love masculinity.)

—There are no such loves today, I say.

—I can believe it, she says. At my age, we understand that. It's because people today get married in haste.

Photographs. Photographs. And more photographs. (One day perhaps I, too, shall love looking at pictures of the dead as much as she does. I shall relive my past by looking at pictures of the dead. It might not be my past, but it is death's past. My father as a young man. The child on his lap. I would miss him. Miss him. I would. One glance at his picture, and I'll see his whole life.)

—Until I was married, my mother had a family

portrait taken every year. If only she had continued this habit, she says.

(And suddenly I can see our own family portraits, though I try to erase them from my mind at once.)

—When I was little, my father would spank me sometimes, she says, pointing at her behind.

—But he always played games with me. He wanted me to have a very good education. When I was older, we became very good friends. The first books he gave me were the Russians. Dostoyevsky and Gogol in particular.

—I never saw his mental anguish. It was something he carried deep inside. My mother used to say it was like milk boiling over. First it bubbles up, and then it overflows.

Now she shows me a picture of Svevo and his wife with a large dog and three puppies.

—This was James Joyce's dog. When he went to Zurich, he asked my father to look after her. No sooner had he left than the dog gave birth. That dog had so much fur that Joyce didn't even realize it was a she. We always had animals. Horses, dogs, and cats.

—Ah, I don't wish to go back to those years. We knew great happiness, but we also suffered great pain. The most painful thing is to lose all your friends. ALL THAT REMAINS IS LONELINESS. WE ARE ALL ALONE.

So says Letizia. Eighty-four years have brought her to this moment, which I share with her under the wondrous lamps in these great marble halls.

Now I have seen all the pictures. The Schmitzes, the Venezianis, Svevo's seven siblings, the painter Veruda, his lover, Joyce's dog. But I have not seen a single picture of the aunts that affected Zeno so deeply.

—Do you have any pictures of your aunts, for instance the one who went to Riga, I say.

—No, we don't have any photographs of her, she says. Uneasily. Unpleasantly.

A dining room.

—We still have our meals here, she says.

This is the last of the chambers.

Today is the thirteenth of July. The time is 10:18. I'm on my way to the Giardino Pubblico in Trieste.

A week ago I was sitting beneath a tree next to Kafka's grave. This park, too, I recognize. The young man in *As a Man Grows Older* spoke of a poor and beautiful girl who lived not far from here. Hadn't she lived in one of the streets off this park, the young woman who had helped him forget Ada and endure his wife.

Here is his grave:

ITALO SVEVO

ROMANZIERE

1861–1928

Across the way is the monument to James Joyce, marking the centenary of his birth:

TRIESTE

A

JAMES JOYCE

NEL CENTENARIO DELLA NASCITA (1882–1982)

Unlike the New Jewish Cemetery in Prague, this park is very lively. The benches are full of Triestines prattling away.

Children are playing. All is alive and well. Svevo's passions. His restless spirit.

Just behind the cemetery, there's an open-air cinema. Tonight they're showing a Dustin Hoffman film.

I sit down on a bench. Look around me. I feel fine. An emaciated old lady is sitting next to me. A young woman has brought her here. Left her to sit here for a while. She takes two small pillows from the plastic bag she's brought with her. She sits on one and puts the other behind her back. So the wooden bench won't crack her bones. She's that frail. Then she puts on dark sunglasses.

She makes me think about myself as an old woman. Such thick blue veins in her hands. When she peers up over her sunglasses, raising her blue-green eyes to the sky, she reminds me of my grandmother.

—Bad weather, she says.

—It might be bad weather for swimming, but it's nice weather for sitting in the park, I say. I'm going to Venice.

—Today, she asks.

—Today, I say.

—Have a good trip, she says.

—Goodbye, I say.

VI

It's the fourteenth of July. A cloudy day.

Last night I was awoken by a tremendous rainstorm, and I remember that while still half-asleep I felt glad to be alive. This is my third night in Trieste and my third hotel. If I decide to stay another day in any city, any country, I change hotels. How much I've longed to live like this, coming and going as I please.

I'm swimming. In waters stretching out to the open sea. I'm so tired I could drown. But I manage to stay in the water for quite a long time, for I've missed the sea so much. This sea smells like the one in Istanbul. The same seaweed in its depths. In my mind's eye I can see the waves foaming as they hit the shore. The hills of Trieste are not as densely populated as the hills along the Bosphorus. They've preserved their green spaces. But viewed from the water, they still call to mind the Asian shore of the Bosphorus. As do these long, long walls. They take you back to the houses on your hill in Arnavutköy, the old wooden houses rising above stone walls like these. These houses are much finer than the ones on your hill. I am lying in the sun. I've lost all my images of the day. My only company my inner voice. This is one of those rare interludes when I am released from unbearable pressure. There was one hotel here in Trieste that had the stench of centuries of accumulation. I listened to songs on the radio. Songs I didn't know, but they sounded beautiful. Because they reminded me of nothing. One lasted almost half an hour. A tale of a wrongful arrest. After that there was a jazz program, as monotonous as music from the Far East, and it lulled me to sleep.

The toothache is almost gone this morning. But I'm still in so much pain that I'm continuing with the pills. My headache has gotten worse, of course. My neck is stiff. I'm wide awake. Every time I move, every part of my body aches. I'm trying to work out where the pain is coming from. Is it the headache I get from the south wind in Istanbul, or the one I get on a cloudy day in Berlin, or the one I get when I'm on the road, or is it one of those migraines that go on for hours and hours. The big sore that sometimes appears on my lower back has reappeared again this morning. What am I so angry about. Apart from myself. Aren't I angry about everything in the world, myself included. Doesn't my anger go beyond anger.

I spend my last hours in Trieste in a café, keeping company with old men and tables, with the streets leading into the square and the square itself, with the cloudy sky and the facades of old buildings, and their windows and their shutters and their ground-floor shops, and the wind, the wind that is bringing more rain. In these final hours that I share with old women, children, and young people, most of them Italians plus a handful of Yugoslavs, one Black man, and many restless pigeons, there is an old woman sitting at the next table, reading a guide to Vienna.

A rough-looking Italian comes over to speak to me. He too says he worked for a time in Germany. Just like the thin-faced woman I met on the bus to Niš Station. He asks me if I can spend one more day in Trieste so we can sleep together. At that moment, and for the first time, the very idea of sex disgusts me.

When I was searching for reflections of my headache in the mirror this morning, there in my third Trieste hotel room, it occurred to me that I carry inside me a spare self, and that it is this spare self that seeks out men—all men, including the Greek. Thinking back to my first husband, and my second husband, and my most recent lover with the beautiful skin, and all the other men I've loved or fucked over the past twenty-five years, it occurred to me that they'd all served a single purpose, which was to help me endure my true self. The closer I come to Turin, the more my thoughts go to Pavese, who was found dead fully dressed in a room, a hotel room. Eleven years, eleven months, and fifteen days ago.

No one has ever touched my heart as he has. In my heart, I know him as my life's greatest love. And now it ignites, my love for this dead man.

As if we were soon to become one in anguish, in impossible, implausible love.

I turn my back on the square where I've just seen my first tramp in Trieste. A thin old man carrying several plastic bags and a big umbrella. He sits down on the stone bench next to the café. Only to stand up right away. His eyes look so lost.

For the first time I can see it in the distance: Santo Stefano Belbo. So I've come the right way. Nothing I see after Santo Stefano Belbo will matter. Will have any significance whatsoever. Will yield a single image I can live with. They can live without me. Other people do not struggle as I do, they do not need another living person at their side to make their way through life. My litany of images will end with his. After Santo Stefano Belbo, this suicide might become my other half. This suicide or Pavese's anguished face. The most anguished face I have ever seen.

I'm on the platform. Standing beside the train that will take me to Turin. The weather is dull and cloudy. Now and again a soft breeze blows in from the sea. No view of the sea from this station.

Today Achim is traveling back from the Southeast. I think of all the stations and countries I've passed through. The thousands of kilometers I've covered by train or on the E5, in his car.

I think of Latislav. I think of him, and I think of Zoran. I think of the young man from Thessaloniki. Of my deathly exhaustion. Of the countless faces I've seen along the way—the children going on vacation with their father, clutching straw hats; the Turkish workers; the West Germans and the East Germans; the Czechs, and Austrians, and Yugoslavs, and Italians—forming and reforming in my mind's eye, beautiful and welcoming, old and fashionable, thin and fat.

I think of Letizia, and of her eighty-four years on this earth. I think of myself, and of the petty bourgeois sentiments against which I have been in lifelong rebellion. Inside which I have so often been contained and constrained. From which I have once again managed to escape. For the duration of this journey, at least, I can drown all those bad memories, all those feelings. I am not a citizen. No country or class can claim me. A modest declaration, but it gives me strength.

I think of my taxi ride from Trieste Central Station to the hotel, so tired I could die. And I think of how, after sleeping for the first time in days, I shall not be seeing the countryside between Trieste and Turin through tired eyes.

Rather than seek to define our surroundings, we must experience them through our senses . . .

No doubt in my mind that Achim has never broken free as much as I have now. In the six weeks that have passed since we sat together on the Havel Busway, waiting for our bus, I have experienced emotions I never knew existed, letting my senses make sense of my surroundings. But I want to wait until I get to Santo Stefano Belbo before I write them down. How often we convince ourselves that things have come to an end, when a lifetime can never be long enough to appreciate life's infinity.

I'm in the third compartment of the carriage going to Turin. The other five seats are empty. I've stretched out my legs so that no one else comes to join me. The carriage is empty. Now the train is traveling along the sea. The sea I swam in yesterday. We come out of the deep-green woodlands. The shore that I thought too vast for people to fill it—this too will soon be behind us. Tomorrow and tomorrow and tomorrow the sun will shine upon this shore again. While I shall look for sunlight in the hills and in the cornfields. Somewhere, anywhere, the night sky will sparkle with stars. Perhaps in Turin first. Stars equal fear.

Before the train departs, a young Italian who works at the station greets me.

—Have a good trip, he says.

—Thank you, I say.

And as I say goodbye it suddenly seems to be that I am leaving a friend behind. I stand up.

There, on platform three, is the young man from Thessaloniki. Looking very tired. He's been searching for me in the crowd, is happy to catch sight of me before my train leaves.

—Did you see the Rolling Stones? I say.

—Yes.

—Were they good?

Strangers always give us so much more of themselves than our friends do. So why don't we spend more of our lives with strangers. Expecting nothing, and never being a burden, free of all those moments we strain to define as happy. To feel nothing—no feeling on earth can be more beautiful. To be numb—so numb as to embrace the world and all humanity.

I lean out the window. Very quickly, I kiss him goodbye. I remember Latislav turning up at the last minute in Prague Main Station.

—I'm going home, he says.

It's clear that he's been meeting every train I might have been taking to Turin. What a cruel old hag I am. I should have faced the realities of femininity some time ago. But this is one thing I've never managed to do.

We keep waving to each other until the moment I sit down and start writing. All the happiness I've found with all the men I've known is equal to the love Letizia found in one man. But to generalize love requires immense discipline. From time to time, when I outstrip myself, I stumble like a young man who is new to all this. Though I have never, ever been new to anything. It has always been clear to me where things begin and end. I live now as I lived in the dull Anatolian towns I knew as a child, cradling life in the palm of my hand, or my mind, or the corner of my eye, and giving my own shape to life as I passed through it, or as it passed me by. Bringing life to the stagnant, and stagnation to life.

Now all I want is for words to leave me be. From that city on the Yugoslavian border. To that city close to the French border. I want to see greenery. I want to see the sea. I want to forget myself. How glad I am that I brought no books with me on this journey. For a quarter century, I've been reading, reading, reading, and now, freed of books, I am looking inside myself for words' traces. I have no time for books or films whose characters and locations are not real but imagined. You can find nothing in them. In every discovery is something never before known.

From time to time, after listening to yet another useless news bulletin, I look out the window at the abandoned vineyards, I think how a life of coincidence is no life at all. And I ask myself if I am really free of coincidences.

Only when I travel am I free of them. The compartment door opens.

—You're sitting all alone here. I thought I'd bring my bag in here so we can talk, says a man.

—I'd rather be alone, I say.

(What a surprise, to hear myself send this man away. Can this be the first time. If I truly wish to be alone, this means that I can no longer endure human company. That I shall spend my time in the Santo Stefano Belbo hills with only mountains and lakes to keep me company, and rivers, trees, and winds, nights and days and clouds and stars and rain and the sky.)

And now, as I travel toward Turin, crossing cornfields and thinking of all the countries I've left behind, I rejoice in my growing independence. My thoughts return to Dostoyevsky, to the days when I first read his books and to the faith they gave me, freeing me to form my own ideas about the world. Far from the powers that forge nations and stage revolutions and sustain wars. If ever I were caught up in a civil war, I would take to the hills like Pavese. For a man who has come into the world to turn his surroundings into poetry, to take up arms and kill is unthinkable. That's why I cannot forgive the Italian progressives who could neither understand nor forgive him.

Just as I cannot forgive the women who accepted his embrace only to reject him. The women who used their sexual inadequacies against him and brought him such pain. As I sit here on this train that is taking me to Turin, at twelve past three on the fourteenth of July, 1982, I know there is nowhere else on earth I would rather be. I have never traveled anywhere with the excitement I now feel as I approach the lands where Cesare Pavese spent his life. Had his suicidal thoughts still lived hidden inside him, I might have had the chance to see his anguished, beautiful face, and who knows, I might have been able to caress it.

We're traveling across cornfields. I am caressed by the train's own breeze. A breeze so much softer than men's hands.

I'm tired. I've lost track of how many times I've passed through Venice. I don't like Venice. Its otherworldly aura. People like me who live outside reality tend to feel uncomfortable in places that look like the surface of the moon or distant planets, or in reality-defying cities like Venice. The void inside me knows no bounds, and this is also why I have such fear of flying.

At Novara I stand up to get a better view of Turin. Just then the drinks cart comes down the corridor.

I order a coffee, wishing to cast off the waves of fatigue that have been passing over me since Milan. The man pushing the drinks cart stops to sit down across from me.

—Why don't you and I go out for a meal tonight in Turin, he says. Then he points to his graying hair.

—I'm getting old, I should be ten years younger. Twenty-nine, he says.

He's different from the other Italians working these trains. He speaks German. English, too. And he's as distraught as any artist.

—I was very young when I packed my bags for Berlin, he says, without my having said a thing. My uncle had a restaurant there. The poor man worked in Berlin for forty years, and now he's buried there.

—But that's life. We all die in the end, he says.

—I had no luck. A lot of the people who went up to Germany with me are rich now. They own their own restaurants. I had no luck, he says.

—No luck with women either, he says.

—I've only ever been lucky at cards. If you don't have a wife or children, you have to find something to do. And for me it's cards.

—I live in Venice now with my parents. For free.

As he relates his life's sorrows in short sentences such as these, he keeps urging me to drink the coffee he's served me. I feel as if I'm talking with one of Pavese's lonely heroes.

—I'm not looking my best right now, but that's because I'm so tired, he says, as he stares gloomily out the window and taps his fingers on his thigh.

(I think of Pavese, who lived all his life with his sister Maria. But always alone.)

We're traveling through the last of the light, it will be night by the time we reach Turin.

And tonight, as soon as we've arrived, I want to walk the streets I know so well from his descriptions. The streets where the loneliest man of our times explored life's deepest depths before committing suicide. The solitary man who was never allowed to love.

How glad I am that it begins to rain as we come into Turin. I love rain and always have. It chimes with my inner life. I fear the loneliness of the night approaching. And after two coffees, I'm wide awake.

VII

Nuto, who stayed, Nuto the carpenter, my ally in those first forays to Canelli, played the clarinet at all the fairs and dances for a good ten years. For ten years his life had been one long party, he knew all the drinkers and the clowns, and all the fun to be had in every village.[12]

It's Friday. Quarter to nine in the morning. I'm in Santo Stefano Belbo. I'm sitting on the concrete roof of Nuto's carpenter shop. He opened up at eight thirty, as he has done for going on sixty years. He turned the lock on his front door six times. There are clocks piled up high in this section. The workshop on the side doubles as Nuto's home. His portrait hangs on one wall, and Pavese's on the wall opposite. I am where I should be.

Lined up along the shelves beneath Pavese's portrait are all his books. His suicidal heroes, his lonely souls—all here. His Turin, his Piedmont. My own loneliness, encircled here by his.

At my feet, a garden planted with saplings. It takes me back to the apple orchards of my childhood.

I try to work out which manner of tree they've planted in this bright patch of green. I cannot. But what I see before me still takes me back to those other apple orchards. When I'd eat only the apples I picked myself, and got so angry whenever my mother would sit me or my sister or brother on her knee to peel our apples for us.

What infuriated me back then was that my mother would always peel apples, but never pears. When my father asked what I loved most, my father or pears.

—Pears, of course, I'd say.

The child inside me thought pears had a taste, an allure, that no father could match. My father would get so angry, you'd think he was the child and I the father. He'd stop with the caresses. What a childish father. That's what the child inside me would think.

My mother's pile of apple peelings would keep on growing. As I sit here in Santo Stefano Belbo, three meters above the ground, surveying the orchards, cornfields, and mountains before me, and the vineyards climbing gentle hills behind me, I see my own childhood memories everywhere engraved. Climbing up onto Nuto's roof, I find it covered with ivy, like the street leading up to my house in Istanbul, like my balcony, which looks out over the Bosphorus.

Faint images drift back to me from childhood and come back into focus: the same plants and trees and grasses and vineyards as I see before me now, the same heady scents and the same light. Sitting here in Santo Stefano Belbo, I am returned to the İzmir countryside that gave me my first images of the world, to that mountain range that gave me my first childhood fears, before spilling into the Aegean Sea.

When Nuto drove past me at eight thirty, the time we had agreed upon the day before, I was just about to write down these words: "Perhaps I came to Santo Stefano Belbo to stop living inside literature. Before I got here, I believed that life was stronger than literature, and I was determined to experience as much of it as I could. But still I could not extract myself from literature, and this was the paradox that held me in its grip."

All those years ago, when I was reading Pavese's *The Moon and the Bonfires* for the first time, I never imagined that I would meet Nuto in the flesh one day, or that I would be getting into his car, a Fiat 126 with this license plate: CN 31 5238. Now I understand that literature has more life in it than life, and that life is its seedbed.

It is in Santo Stefano Belbo that I come to understand why I have been with so many men. I was so afraid of losing myself inside my unbounded world that I found comfort in the bounded worlds of others. But immersed as I am now in my own unbounded world, and understanding it better than ever before, I am determined to leave that fear behind. How much better, to carry your own burdens through life, instead of someone else's.

JOURNEY TO THE EDGE OF LIFE

I have traveled the world enough by now to know that there is good in every living person, and that we are all alike.[13]

Just before the train pulls into Turin, the drinks-cart man comes back. He's taken off his work apron and combed his gray hair.

We're both the same age. He calls himself old, and I call myself ageless.

He's slapped on a lot of cologne to make me like him. Though he knows he has no luck with women, he's still trying. He's also brought a can of Peroni.

Nuto is sitting in the shade, beneath the ivy, reading his paper. I'm thirsty. He stands up. Steps out in front of me. We go into the quadrant where he has his carpentry workshop, and over to the quadrant where he has his counter. In the dark hallway leading to the stairs that go up to the top floor, there is a large pile of old newspapers. The shop's fourth quadrant is a windowless room where Nuto stores everything he has collected for going on a century. Pavese's empty red-wine bottles must certainly be in there somewhere.

Now I understand: it is people like Nuto who create literature and people like Nuto who keep it alive.

He turns the crank of the water pump. Ice-cold spring water flows into the overgrown garden behind the workshop.

—Drink it slowly, he says.

Nuto's wisdom is drawn from both nature and reason and has served him well for many long years. He retrieves a bottle from the cobwebs and washes it for me.

He gives me water, and a glass.

Together we glance at the newspaper. Israel's war on the Palestinians is continuing. The Germans have launched a new missile cutter in Kiel. There's a picture of it in the paper. Bijola, Nuto's eight-year-old dog, no longer barks at me when I walk past.

Pavese the intellectual respected Nuto as an artisan, and perhaps that is why he called his diaries *Il mestiere di vivere,* "the craft of living."

The drinks-cart man pours beer into two plastic cups.

—Do you like it with foam, or without, he asks.

Here I am, a woman he hopes to seduce, and he's talking like a waiter in his uncle's restaurant.

We clink cups. Being plastic, they don't make a sound. It breaks my heart to see how unhappy he is to be unlucky with women. He can't even get his glasses to clink. He knows it's hopeless. He turns to the window, glowering. He's invited a woman out for supper, and he can't even look at her.

Because I've mentioned wanting a hotel room with a radio, he shows me his:

—Grundig, he says. I bought it in Germany

After asking me what my name is and where I'm from, he says the most intelligent thing I've heard so far:

—So you speak another language.

—I've traveled to many countries, too, he says.

—They eat pasta and pizza all over the world. In Copenhagen. Even in London.

He carries my bag as far as the station's front hall. Still

hoping to forget how little luck he has with women, if only for a few hours.

He tells me to wait there until he's picked up the drinks he'll be selling on tomorrow's train. This time from Turin to Venice.

Venice, where he lives with his parents for free but lacks a woman. I've run out of pity for him. If he knows that people all over the world eat pasta, he must also know to take responsibility for his loneliness—that is his to carry.

As soon as he has vanished into the crowd, holding his radio in one hand and his drinks list in the other, I make a run for it. Lest the loneliness in his eyes be contagious.

Crossing the road outside the station, I see a boulevard stretching out before me, a tree-lined boulevard that I recognize from Pavese's books. It must be the one he spent so much time walking up and down, whenever he was in Turin.

It's as if we're soon to meet at a corner café, there to leave our lonely shells behind. Back when I was reading his books in Istanbul, I imagined a city with the grand boulevards and squares that I associated with all European cities. Cities like Trieste. But Turin strikes me at once as a city that frightens and oppresses. Though it's possible that I'm imagining such an atmosphere, knowing, as I do, that this is where he committed suicide. But I already knew of all this from my very first encounters with his world: his little joys, his life-long suffering, and his longing for death. I cross the street with these thoughts in mind. I stop in front of the reception desk in the Hotel Bologna.

Again I shudder, thinking that this could be the hotel where he killed himself. I've never seen a hotel with such long corridors. Corridors as long as the ones in Kafka's *The Castle*. As long as fear, and nightmares. On and on they go, to the end of life. If I saw this in a dream, I would wake up screaming. On each floor, a new and dark kilometer to travel. Past piles of dirty sheets. Spare cots in every corner. There's paint peeling off the ceiling in the room they want to give me.

—It's very stuffy in here, I say.

I imagine a dead body beneath the piles of dirty laundry. The corpses of guests driven to suicide.

I return to the boulevards. Lit up for the night and packed with summer crowds. My fear fades away. I decide to go deeper into the city. The cafés are full. My rolling suitcase is making its terrible noise. Attracting glances from the cafés. I don't care at all, though. As I search for a hotel that won't suffocate me, I am—I decide—also putting a distance between myself and his death. I am walking now in the streets where he spent his nights, and what I most want to know is which of these cafés he liked the most, where it was that he most liked to write.

The young man at the Hotel Roma reception desk is more attuned to Pavese than the ones in his old office at the Einaudi publishing house.

—He was a very pessimistic writer, he says.

—Literature is born of pessimism, I say.

Stepping into a lift that resembles an upright coffin and rising into darkness. The lift has the dimensions of a coffin, too. But this one was made for a body larger than Pavese's. Today, as I sit on the concrete roof of Nuto's carpentry shop, writing these words, I am thinking that Pavese saw in this coffin a road to death. His last road. To suicide. There is no lift darker or more enclosed, or more conducive to suicide. It is not just in his novels and poems and diaries that you can find Pavese's suicide reflected. It is also reflected in his surroundings, in the boulevards he walked up and the avenues he walked down and the pavements he crossed. It has left its traces in the Turin station, and the square in front, in the name of the hotel where he took his life, and in its corridors, lifts, and rooms. As fully as he lived his life in Turin, and in Santo Stefano Belbo, the town of his birth, he must also have lived his suicide. Preparing for it, rehearsing it, living it in this nightmare of dark and mystical spaces. In Santo Stefano Belbo there are no sights that might carry a person to his death. All is bright there, all is clear. That is why he went back to Santo Stefano Belbo so often before he died. Nuto, his friend the carpenter, his manual laborer, is in Santo Stefano Belbo. Even today. And in sixty-three minutes he will once again open his workshop's wooden doors, the doors behind which he still lives as Pavese's extension. You could say that part of Pavese lives on inside Nuto, or that part of Nuto died with Pavese. The Hotel Roma is on the other side of the square from the Turin station. The station from which he set out on so many of his journeys. The station to which he always returned. When he went to Canelli, or to Roma, or to Calabria, where he was exiled, he started out in this square. Piazza Felice, as they call it. Happy Square. When he returned from exile, still hoping that "the woman with the hoarse voice" might accept his hand in marriage, it must have been on this square that he found out she had married someone else. I could walk these streets all night. That might make my first night in Turin easier. Here in this city, I can't stop thinking about his suicide. I find its atmosphere frightening. Its streets forlorn. There is something about this city that pulls a person down. Something in its hidden depths that speaks of suicide, that pines for it.

I am very tired by the time two young men come to walk alongside me. I have no idea where to go. My first impression of them is that they know little of life and are content with small talk.

One of the young men takes charge of my bag, and at around eleven thirty I find a room for myself in the Hotel Venezia on Via XX Settembre.

At the entrance is a pale little woman as old as the ages, drifting off to sleep.

Across from the Albergo dell'Angelo—his name for the hotel where he stayed when traveling between Turin and Santo Stefano Belbo—there is another hotel called the Roma. He must have traveled up and down the lift of the Hotel Roma, must have noticed that it looked like a coffin. The corridors of the Hotel Roma are even longer than those of the Hotel Bologna. Darker and more stifling. Dark, long, airless, lonely, bitter, cruel. Corridors that offer no way back from death. Room 305, the room where he took his life, is at the very end of the suicide corridor. Its window looks out over Piazza Felice.

13:24. I move into the shade. I drink my water, which the sun has heated up to sixty degrees. The bench I'm sitting on has been here since Nuto was a child. He must have sat here, too. Nuto alone keeps his world as it is. And he is who he is. As I make the short trip from the roof to the shade of the vines, I tell myself, "You think you're like Dostoyevsky's Grushenka, but there's more to it than that. You're a djinn, a djinn!"

I am on my way to room 305. Following the man from the reception desk. A slim and sweet-natured young man. So fragile that if I so much as touched him, he would break. This is a room like any other. Neither stuffy nor stifling. Neither big nor small. Neither sunny nor dark. Neither living nor dead. Not a whiff of death here. But also, not a whiff of life. It's that kind of room. It chases away all the corridor's dark associations. It leaves me cold. This room has been renovated. It carries no traces of Pavese's last day. When my guide opens another door, I am expecting to see a bathroom or a closet. We step into darkness. This room's shutters are closed. Even in this darkness, I can feel the walls closing in. And that is not all. In this dark and narrow room, I see suicide. The distance between us closes. He wraps his being around mine. My life in time, and forever. His suicide eternal. And I, in its eternal embrace. If I were alone here, I would collapse. I would lie down on this bed. Scream. Cry. Here it is, then. Death. Death in all its shapes. This is the room. This is the coffin. The cemetery that the Hotel Roma keeps hidden, in room 305.

The same bedstead as in the photograph, it must be. The bed where they found Pavese, fully dressed. At a time when I was still in the wheat fields, trying to see the world . . .

> *To become fully human, now that is another matter. It calls for luck, courage, and desire. It calls for the courage to live as if no one else in the world existed. To think only of what you wish to do. Never fearing that others might not care. You need to wait for years, you need to die. And if your luck holds after death, then you might be something.*

Other things left from that day in that room: a wooden chest with four drawers. A bedside table and a chair. These are the remnants that take me back into his last evening. The floor and ceiling and walls have all been renovated. The room would have been much shabbier back then. The door behind the bed leads to the bathroom.

—Does the hotel ever put its guests here.

—It's part of room 305. No one thinks of it as the room where Pavese took his life. RAI did a film once. Hardly anyone comes to see this room. I've been working in this hotel for four years, and you're the first visitor who's asked to see it.

He must have come to visit this secret cemetery in room 305 beforehand. He didn't just come here to die alone, but also to prepare for death. These are places where he spent long hours thinking: Piazza Felice, the Hotel Roma, the lift, the corridor, the secret cemetery in room 305. This was a suicide long contemplated on his many long and solitary summer evenings in Turin. The summer evenings he spent alone, in this murderous city.

I am entering the underpass when the hotel receptionist catches up with me:

—I'm on my lunch break.

I'm glad to see this young man who came with me into the death room. He helps me buy my ticket for Santo Stefano Belbo. Searching the hundreds of arrivals and departures on the board, he finds me a train that will be leaving at 14:00 from platform one. I'm so far outside myself. I hardly know where I am. He walks with me to the Hotel Venezia. How young he is, how alive. Even in death, I can see that. He has a few gray hairs. They suit his youthful face. I might almost be walking through the dead July heat of this deadening city with Cesare Pavese.

I pack up my things. I'm tired. I haven't brought much with me, but it still takes me an hour. I've brought two extra irons. (On my next journey, I shall bring two extra radios.)

At 13:00, I sit down with the old woman who is again at the hotel entrance, waiting for the evening. She wakes up, to search me with her bright blue eyes.

Protected from the bright midday light of Via XX Settembre, the hotel entrance is cool.

—Who are you?

—I am me.

—I know you're you. But what's hiding there behind you?

—Why do I see you here every time I enter or leave this hotel?

—I'm sitting here.

—I know you're sitting here, but why?

—I live here.

—Have you lived here all your life?

—Have you ever worked?

—I did.

—Husband?

—He died in 1975.

—Don't you have any children?

—I had one son, last winter, on the twenty-third of January, he committed suicide.

(She says *suicide* in French.)

—Where?

—In Turin.

—How?

—In his car. Carbon monoxide.

—Why?

—Love, she says, in a voice as deep as her 159 years.

—I have a new love for every new day.

—You do well.

Then we talk about Paris and art. I mention visiting Matisse's house in Nice. I'm about to say I prefer Matisse to Picasso when she says the same thing.

—Matisse is Matisse, she says in her singsong voice, giving his grand name its due. "The tears of the world are a constant quantity. For each one who begins to weep somewhere else another stops." As I write down these words by Beckett in the shade of Nuto's gazebo, I start changing them around. "There is no end to stories on this earth. When one person's story comes to an end, another person somewhere else starts another." "There is no end to suicide on this earth. When one person starts to die, another person in another place starts to live."

When I reach the station a few minutes before two o' clock, I know that Orazio will be waiting for me. Before the train leaves, he kisses me. His facial muscles trembling with excitement. And at that moment, I am once again a young girl with my whole life ahead of me. And that is when I understand that I am not the only one to begin anew with each new day, that the young people sitting across from me can sense this in me, are themselves searching for life's secrets, have joined me here because they know me to be a woman who brings her past and her new beginnings into every new moment.

VIII

July 17, 21:39
Santo Stefano Belbo
Albergo dell'Angelo

In the dream where I saw Christa standing at the head
    of the bed
Christa standing at the head of the bed, telling me she
    had to die
And me seeing how much longer her hair was, in my dream
How pale she was
As pale as death, in my dream
Süm and I sitting side by side on a wooden bench
A wooden bench facing her bed
A wooden bench identical to the bench on which Achim
    and I waited for our bus at the Havel Busway
A wooden bench facing her bed in that hospital with

marble floors
In my dream, while Süm and I cannot bring ourselves to watch Christa die
Death stands at the head of the bed
Deathly pale and thin, her hair long
Her tiny hands clutching the iron bedstead
At the moment when she has to die
In this hospital room as I watched it stretch into infinity, to embrace all life
In the dream where you showed me that everything under the sun, even marble, knows no bounds
The dream where Christa saw what cannot be seen, at the moment she had to die
Head bowed on a bed turned to the wall
Standing at the head of the bed, at the moment she had to die, in my dream
Süm and I, shying away from the moment when she had to die
Running away, leaving Achim to face it alone, in my dream.

IX

July 17–18, 2:36
Santo Stefano Belbo

I was heading back to Rosa's house at around eleven last night when I jumped away from a shadow that turned out to be my own. I was frightened. Frightened of myself. This fear I know I can conquer.

My mind goes back to the dull Anatolian towns of my childhood, when I'd look at the shadow that never stopped following me, all day long. Another image coming into focus here in Santo Stefano Belbo. The deathly, all-conquering light beating down on us on a summer's day. How it frightened me. Now and again, it still does. The bright light of summer can still destroy me. Wherever I happen to be. Moments when I shrink into the silent depths, smothered by the sun's relentless rays. These, then, are the moments when I die.

JOURNEY TO THE EDGE OF LIFE

The day's lovely warmth soon to end.

A day spent basking in it, never getting enough of it, but this evening is still balmy.

I lie in bed for two hours, drifting in and out of sleep. Somewhere out in the garden, that dog is still barking. First I thought it was a woman screaming, but for the past three nights, I've been thinking it must be a dog. Definitely not a chicken. Though it could be a turkey.

I give up on sleep.

On Saturday Orazio came down from Turin to see me, and we talked all day long. We met in Piazza Umberto I at ten o'clock. I'm glad he's come to see me.

A beautiful Saturday morning. So much to look forward to. Youth, warmth, Nuto, vineyards, the house where he was born. New to my touch: Orazio's skin. Lovely cafés. The town's smiling people. The joy all this brings me. How good to be alive. We go first to see the bust of Pavese, which stands between the primary and middle schools. His anguished face, once again before me. I ignore the schools, because I hate all schools.

On the road to Canelli, in front of the cemetery, Orazio kisses me.

—Why did you come after me, I ask.

(It's the first question I've asked him.)

—What moment pushed you toward me.

—The moment when we stood together in room 305.

—Which room 305. The front room, or the cemetery room.

—The room where he committed suicide. You were

staring so hard at that wooden bedstead that I had to come after you.

This is not the answer I was expecting.

Later, as we make love in the vineyard, it is very hot. There on the ground on this sloping vineyard, in the baking July sun, his young and unloved body bears no resemblance to my own. But is it not my unquenchable thirst, is it not the ravenous and ever-growing hunger spilling out of me, that I see reflected on unloved bodies.

—Am I the first woman you've even been with?

(Another first question.)

—The second, he says. I slept with a virgin in Calabria.

(Why Calabria, his place of exile.)

I wrap my arms around him and pleasure myself in the sun. Under the sun's endless warmth, at this moment so full of youth, life, suicide, and death. Under the sun of Santo Stefano Belbo, a beautiful finish.

Pursing his thin little lips:

—I did it all wrong, he says.

—No, you were fine, I say.

—Don't forget this. Many women come after a man has withdrawn, and not when his organ is still inside. A man can go in and out of a woman to his heart's content, but all he will give her is proof of his masculine power. He will never give her that short and longed for moment of beautiful death. This is probably the most painful aspect of male-female relations. A woman must rush to orgasm, if she is to experience it at the same time as you.

Later, when we are sitting under a tree with Nuto. Nuto:

—Did you meet at the Hotel Roma, he says.

—Yes, and we love each other, I say.

—This is a new thing then, Nuto says.

—These are new times, too new to be understood, I say.

At six minutes to five in the morning, there's a storm. Lightning flashing on my face through the gaps in the shutters. Terrifying. Terrifying to hear the sky crack open out here in these hills. This is different from lightning in a big city. It crashes against each peak, and from there it rises, rises. Like the thunder I knew as a child. That we both knew as children, living the same lives under the same conditions.

The creature is screeching again.

My first night in this house, it was the cicadas that woke me up. For hours and hours, I listened to the night. After that I slept so deeply I thought I must have drugged myself. Until I had that dream about Christa. I could see death so clearly then that tonight I cannot sleep at all. While I listen to the rain pour down like water from a glass, I pass the time by thinking about the world of summer. Rain gets right inside me. My closest friend, come to teach me about nature and the world.

To Hemingway:

Have you ever seen the mountains of Piedmont? They're brown and yellow and misty, these parts. And sometimes green. If you saw them, you'd love them.

Yours, C. P.[14]

I think about Hemingway, whose life also ended in suicide. And I think about Pavese, who divided his life between Turin, Santo Stefano Belbo, and Rome.

This is how I pass my sleepless night.

Orazio is staying in another house. The townspeople did everything they could to make sure that he slept on one slope, while I enjoyed the thunder on the other.

We're boarding the 9:53 train to Turin. He has to start work at the Hotel Roma at 14:00.

5:16. Almost morning. It's started to rain. The room is still hot. I'm sweating.

"Langhe." The story I translated many years ago. It holds the seeds of his novel, *The Moon and the Bonfires*. And it was this story that took me to Langhe.

No photograph of "the woman with the hoarse voice" at Nuto's. How I would have loved to walk through the vineyards in the rain.

Rosa comes to my room. Asks why I'm not asleep.

—I'm working, I say.

She asks where I'd like to eat.

(I won't be eating here again.)

She asks me when I'm coming back to the house. She asks where I'll be eating tomorrow.

—Today I'm heading back to Turin, I say.

Rosa is seventy years old. She lives alone in this apartment. Her daughters live in Santo Stefano Belbo too. When she talks, she shouts louder than I do. She's very thin. She has a rosary hanging in each window, a color photograph of the pope on each mirror, and an illustration of Mary nursing Jesus over each bed.

She's standing before me in her white lace nightgown.
—This sort of handwork is back in style, she says.
She tries on my shoes.
—My feet are size thirty-eight.
I ask her if that's an animal screeching in her garden, and if so what kind.
—It's a peacock, she says.
—We've had people from Russia, and Japan, and New Zealand, says Nuto. But you are the first one from Turkey to come here for Pavese.

Where do I come from. Is it the hills of the Bosphorus. Is it Prague. Is it the cemeteries of my world of literature. The neighbors are talking. How lovely it is, to hear morning conversations after a sleepless night. Rosa is up again.

—Such lovely rain that was. Dear God, what lovely rain. It's Mother Mary again, giving us water.
—Do you understand, she asks.
—Jesus Christ, I say.

Santo Stefano Belbo is still in the Middle Ages. How I love these people at moments like these, when I am drifting outside time, beset by deathly thoughts. So much life in them, enough to pull me back.

This neighborhood is overrun by cars, like the rest of Italy, and it has plenty of new buildings, but Nuto still insists on preserving the old. His workshop is full of violins, double basses, cellos, and violoncellos. He made them all himself. The table with the snake legs, too. He's covered it with a tablecloth. When he pulls it off, I see that he's engraved the score for Schubert's "Ave Maria" into the wood.

—Pavese loved Vivaldi and Beethoven, he says.
—I come in here to kill time, he says.
—My life ended long ago.
—Life never ends, I say.

It's afternoon. I'm sitting in the shade of Nuto's gazebo. Nuto, Orazio, Bijola, and me. Two funeral corteges pass before us. Each has a separate car for the flowers. Followed by a long line of cars, as I read the following lines in a newspaper dated August 28–29, 1950:

GAZZETTA SERA

28–29 AGOSTO 1950

20 LIRE

On the left-hand side of the front page, a report on the suicide. He arrives at the hotel at 20:30. He swallows twenty-two sleeping pills.

He is found dead on that wooden bedstead, wearing his suit. He'd only taken off his shoes.

I embrace you all and apologize to you all. No words. Only actions. I shall never write again.[15]

He is found by a maid at eight thirty the next morning when she enters the room with a cat.

On the right-hand side of the front page is more news from the White House:

This is what Truman has to say: "If Vienna is lost, it means all of Europe is lost. If Vienna is saved, it means all of Europe is saved."

JOURNEY TO THE EDGE OF LIFE

The third news item on this page: the Reds of North Korea declare victory in Daegu.

(This makes me think of my own countrymen who died on the Korean front, heroic soldiers with no idea where they were. My first encounter with war. Only my thin, wizened grandmother spoke of war as a bad thing. We children played at American Brothers in the streets. The workers of Turin announce that they'll be on strike on the fourth of September.)

....

An earthquake in India: eighty dead.

Dante Spada, a thief better known as Tarzan, has been arrested in Nice.

....

Two Bulgarian ministers have been sentenced to life imprisonment, while others were given sentences ranging between eight and fifteen years.

....

In the Turin cinemas where Pavese went to kill time, these films are showing on the night of his suicide:

Undertow
Scott Brady, John Russell, Dorothy Hart
Universal International

Malaya
Spencer Tracy, James Stewart
MGM

Francis the Talking Mule
Donald O'Connor
Universal International

—Just look at that, says Nuto, directing my attention and Orazio's to the funeral procession.

"Death is nothing. Nothing at all." Svevo's last words to his daughter.

But suicide.

IX

Orazio wants to give me room 305. I take room 221. I'm one floor below and my room looks out onto a side street and not Piazza Felice. The first thing I do is hang his mournful portrait on the back of the door. After that I close the door to the balcony and then all the shutters. On the radiator I place photographs of his Santo Stefano Belbo.

At nine in the morning, Orazio and I head to the station. The rain on the streets has yet to evaporate. The townspeople are preparing for Sunday mass. My friends the elderly gentlemen are dressed in their best suits. Their most perfectly ironed shirts. They're wearing ties. Are freshly shaven. Old men, young women, and children, all alight with a sense of occasion.

After mass, Nuto will take his wife to the Albergo dell'Angelo for lunch, as he does every Sunday. A tradition unbroken over half a century. Happy people, living out their lives in a single village.

Nuto, and all these men, young and old, all the people of Santo Stefano Belbo, all of them, Rosa and all the hills of Piedmont, its vineyards and houses, its stone bridge over the river and its rumbling sky, its old mansions and singing cicadas and summer storms—this world that reached out to me, came all the way to Istanbul. I shall keep this world inside me. And I'll be back. One day I shall meet again with Rosa on the dirt path that runs along the banks, as she makes her way to mass.

Leaving the Turin station, we take the pedestrian crossing to the far side of the square. Walking under the galleries until we reach the Hotel Roma. Once inside, we step again into the lift that resembles a coffin. My room has been thoroughly renovated. Not a trace of suicide here. But isn't it one floor up, that suicide, at the dead end of a long and dark corridor. Am I savoring this pain. Why can't I tear myself away from this hotel. Why am I not back on the tracks with a speeding train.

The time is half past two.

At five, I pick up the phone.

—I've had some sleep, Orazio, I say.

I put down the phone.

The phone rings.

—I forgot to tell you how wonderful you are, says Orazio. And immediately, he hangs up.

An hour later, I am standing next to Orazio. In the lift, I think of the words Achim wrote on the inside cover of *An Absurd Vice*. ("We bought this for you last year. Back when we couldn't find the words for Christa. Now those words are digging deep holes into my heart." Achim. The end of March, 1982.) I pick up the phone to call my old friend Achim. If you were here, we could go together to Platti, Pavese's café.

Platti is a corner café where everything remains as it was in 1880. I'm drinking tea at one of the small outside tables, in the gallery's cavernous shade. There on the corner that I recognized at once when I first left the Turin station, where a side street crosses with this avenue that I came to know so intimately from his books and have seen in so many dreams. Reliving his many long walks. I count the steps between Platti and the Einaudi publishing house, where he worked for so many years. First turn right onto Corso Giacomo Matteotti, and then onto Via San Quintino, and finally onto Via Umberto Biancamano. The publishing house is the first building. A six-story building. Three hundred and seventy steps from here to Platti.

Between the café and the Hotel Roma, 598 steps. Steps 270 and 430 cut across the tram tracks that pass beneath the galleries before turning onto side streets. The road runs along the shops that line the dark covered galleries.

Einaudi, Caffè Platti, Hotel Roma: 968 steps in all. This is a city closed off from the sky. Channeling its traffic through concrete galleries that lead on to marble galleries that block the rain and wind and clouds. This city bears some responsibility for his suicide. I'm surprised that he never described it as oppressive. He must have been so deep inside his suicidal thoughts that he never saw this. It's 12:12.

Orazio has finished his shift. He's here with me now. He takes off his glasses. Glasses that make his black eyes look so much deeper. He's going to take a shower, before sleeping with a woman for the third time in his twenty-one years of life. With the woman I am watching.

No morning light seeping into the room. This is the first time Orazio has ever spent a whole night with a woman. Knowing there will never be a next time, you have undertaken to usher him through all your body's gates and passages.

You think how oppressed people in this country are by the laws of marriage and religion. The sanctity of a Catholic marriage—this, too, must have pushed him toward suicide. You wonder how many of the women he slept with were truly women. If they ever understood that a man could only feel strong if they themselves felt truly female, if they knew they had the power to give a man's power the shape they themselves desired.

As for his last novel, *The Moon and the Bonfires*. You wonder if he set down his last words too soon. If this book was before its time. If someone lives to write, what does he do once he knows that there is nothing left to write.

I shall write no more. I shall be as stubborn as the people of Langhe as I journey toward the land of the dead.

Turin, nineteenth of July, Parco del Valentino. 16:00.

These gardens, too, are as I imagined them. This row of garden taverns skirting the banks of the Po, these towering old trees, with their thick trunks and pale leaves—they have not changed since his day. These little establishments are the same as they were in 1950. These tables, these chairs, these gardens. This is where that lonely man would while away his long summer evenings, waiting, longing, for a girl—a waitress, a dancer—to show an interest. Hadn't he once waited long hours in the rain for a girl just in front of these gardens, soaked through but still waiting for this girl who never came, hadn't he fallen gravely ill that same night.

It's not just his anguish and despair and loneliness that I share with him and take inside me as I survey these gardens. These trees, their leaves fading but still green, still timeless. Now as then, still waiting for lost time, still pressing down, down, down.

Nowhere have I seen gardens that speak so powerfully of loneliness as these. Not even in the Stockholm suburbs. There's something about this place. A secret sort of death. A force that I struggle to name or define amid this greenery, a force that he should have run away from and did not run away from, that instead fired up his suicidal thoughts.

Of course these gardens remind me of the Istanbul Municipal Gazino, where my mother, like all upright mothers, took me as a child. We'd go there with other children and their ugly mothers, and how very bored I'd be. I, a child. One of the other children later fell prey to schizophrenia, suffering for many years. Another joined the fascists and was killed in a wave of terror. He too suffered from mental illness for many years. By the time he finished university, he looked like an old man. Not long afterward, he was killed, somewhere near the Black Sea. As a child he had a broad forehead and a big head.

—These days I've spent with you have been extraordinary, says Orazio.

He's stroking my hair.

The rain has stopped. The sun darts in and out of the clouds. But clouds still cover most of the sky.

Music playing in some of the taverns. Not even music can bring life into these gardens. It only adds to the melancholy. If Orazio weren't here with me, I would collapse into my anguish. All this green, it speaks only of suicide.

It is now, here in Turin, in the Parco del Valentino, that I at last understand why I was so unhappy as a child. Within childhood's terrifying limits. Inside childhood's cold nights. Its images, narrow, still, and impossible. Its formidable walls. The terrifying consequences, when adults think themselves adults, dismissing children as children. Permitting no child to stray beyond the boundaries imposed on childhood. I understand now that I see the world today as I saw it then—through the same eyes, thinking the same thoughts. The same insights and feelings. All that happened with the passage of years was that they grew, they accumulated. Became too many and varied for me to bear. But I am no longer a prisoner of childhood. No longer childhood's exile. To be a child is to be in prison. To be a child is to be exiled from the world. As here, in Turin. A city I must flee. If I do not wish to travel to the world of the dead, I must leave at once.

I see now that the only hope for happiness in the Parco del Valentino is to leave. To leave everything. All our childhoods, all our pain, all our love, all our insatiable longings, all our nights and days and marriages and family ties, all our new moons and countries and borders and habits, from all our worlds and all other worlds, too, from all lives. Every night I die. Then I rise from the dead to live again. Every twenty-four hours, every life, every death. And for the first time since I embarked on this journey, to wander the streets and boulevards and cafés and cemeteries and houses of my beloved writers—this journey through their worlds, as they saw them—I can feel the two warring selves inside me merge into one. Sometimes I see eternity as a light, sometimes as a gray line. But didn't the child see that same light in Esentepe.

June 20, 8:36

The train has just left the Turin station. And Orazio, standing on platform seventeen in his white shirt and navy trousers. His dark black eyes. His arms, so slender. His body, so narrow. His lips, so thin. Standing still on platform seventeen. Until he vanishes into the distance with the Hotel Roma.

I'm passing through the Turin suburbs. Soon the cornfields will start.

That day I stopped in the cornfields to listen to the rustling leaves. As the stalks swayed in the wind that day, I remembered something. Something I'd long ago forgotten. Beyond these fields, beyond those other fields rising up into the hills, there was the sky, the empty sky.

That great man, so alone. This damned and damning world.

How I love him.

Yesterday I went to stand in front of his sister's house. Corso Giovanni Pascoli 9. I rang the bell for Sini/Pavese several times. A large building with five entrances. In a new part of town. What a terrible thing to see: these hundreds of windows, reflecting the hundreds of families huddled inside them. To think of Maria, aged eighty-four, sitting there in the bright summer sun. She lives here with her daughter. Her daughter never married. First she looked after her father, and now she's looking after her mother. I am thinking of Pavese's novel, *Among Women Only*. Some people have patience, others do not. I am one of the latter. As I stand before this great big building, I am for the first time glad about his suicide. Glad that he never had to live here, never had to move out to the city's new neighborhoods, to these streets, these houses. How it frightens me, the harsh light reflecting off them. Why should anyone have to endure this life any longer. Endure such loneliness any longer. Endure this bright and timeless light. Why should he carry any longer this yearning for suicide, which he has borne since the moment of his birth.

God endowed me with great gifts. To others he gave cancer.

Some he made fools. Some he sent to death when they were still children. God in his greatness works in mysterious ways. Here are five thousand lire. For the priest in Castellazzo. Let him tell his own stories. Let him hear them for himself. Let us hope at least that he believes what he says.

Look at yourselves. When I do so, I feel like a fish in a block of ice.[16]

After writing this letter, he goes to *L'Unità*, the newspaper he writes for.

He chooses for himself the photograph that will accompany the news of his death. This is a suicide planned slowly and lived over many years.

CIMITERO PRINCIPALE.

The faint yellow light I've seen reaching to eternity—now I see it stretching for kilometers along these cemetery walls. No sight has ever surprised me as much as this one. (Up until now, I've never dared to visit a concentration camp.)

A sight I could never have dreamed or imagined. Would I find a Catholic heaven beyond those gates. Silence. No visitors, except for me. Little box graves lined up along walls many kilometers long. On every grave, a photograph of the deceased. In front of each headstone, a vase. In every vase, a plastic flower. On they go, these graves, these box graves, with their photographs of the deceased and their plastic flowers. Along the walls that enclose the courtyard. As far as the eye can see. I cannot even imagine a city's heavy breath in the beyond. How glad I am that he's not resting here between these walls, where I can see to the other side of death. His grave is in the inner courtyard. Green marble. In the marble vases that stand on either side, immaculate plastic hydrangeas. His photograph is here, too. But why do I find this cemetery, these plastic hydrangeas, this heavy marble, so alien to the man he was and the words he left us. Why do I wish to see him only in the Piedmont hills, close to the earth and the rustling cornfields, in a grave not yet turned to stone.

It was late in the afternoon when I set out with Orazio for a stroll through Parco del Valentino. Caught by a sudden shower, we take refuge beneath the roof of one of the taverns. I look around me, at the tables and chairs from another age. Some way away, a young man is reading a book. I wanted him to be reading Pavese. But he's reading Nietzsche's *Thus Spoke Zarathustra*.

I gaze at the Po through the old trees' melancholy branches. At the great raindrops bouncing on the face of the water. Intimations of another world. When the rain has stopped, we continue along the asphalt path running alongside the taverns. Orazio is holding my hand. Steam rises from the asphalt. We touch it, and it's hot.

—It's beautiful here, says Orazio.

Later, when we're standing on Umberto I Bridge, I capture the one image of this city that lets me breathe.

No. No. This city was built in the wrong place. It should have been built along the river, to rise up into these hills. No city was ever designed to induce suicidal thoughts more than this one. No other city could push a person this far. No city on earth. It's shut off from the mountains. From the Po, the sun, the rain, the stars, the breeze. From all that is open and wide. It's impossible to breathe here. It hides itself behind those galleries that close off the sky. Those lamplit galleries with their marble floors and thick, heavy stone columns, their old-world coffeehouses and opulent stores. Opening out from time to time onto squares decked with eerie, weighty sculptures and gigantic stone lions. There are no people in these squares. The plaster on the grand old edifices darkened by time and bearing time's unbearable weight. I look up the staircase of the first house he lived in, on Via XX Settembre. A faint light seeps in from the courtyard. Beyond, all is darkness.

From across the street I look at his last address. Via Lamarmora 35. With every breath I take, his suicide repeats itself. It's from here that he sets out for the Hotel Roma. Every avenue closed in on itself. Every building. Every stone. Every marble slab paving the way beneath the galleries. Those who built this city were enemies of the natural world, of mountains and the sun, of the gray clouds turning with the seasons, of rivers and the sky, of rain and the blue beyond, and the caressing winds. They've turned nature into stone. They've locked humankind inside a world where nothing can live that has not been shaped by their hands. The wooden doors along these galleries open into the haunted corridors of old buildings. Nothing in these buildings or their endless corridors is fit for human life. And this city woven from fear finds its terminus on the third floor of the Hotel

Roma. Which is served, to this day, by the same lift that sent him on his final journey. You step out of the lift to feel your way down an unlit corridor. You open the door. Behind the large room you see before you, the secret room awaits. The suicide room, with the same bedstead. Have you come to this corridor to relive his suicide. You have been going up and down the same lift.

I must go. I must go. I must go. I must go. I must go. And as I go, as I make my way or the train makes its way through landscapes, towns, villages, and cornfields, around mountain ranges and along the shores of lakes, along riverbeds or gray seas—as people I don't know vanish into the distance, as they fade away with every new image, fade into empty space—only then do I move away from the edge of life. And from its beginning. I must go. Leave his suicide where it is, at the end of the corridor, in the secret chamber adjoining room 305. Parco del Valentino, the lonely nights, the galleries, the trees so heavy and so green, the cemetery walls, so long, so yellow, so pale, *The Moon and the Bonfires*—they fade away. The creaky little lift, the despair, the suicidal passion—it all ends there. As loneliness loses shape. Surrenders to a greater loneliness. To nothingness. And *isn't life only the wind, only the sky, only the leaves, and only nothing.*

Berlin, August 1982
Arnavutköy, February 1984

Translator's Note

The Turkish Republic went to great lengths in the middle decades of the twentieth century to stamp out all but one of the languages it had inherited from the Ottoman Empire. Citizens Speak Turkish was the name of the official campaign. But the Istanbul of Tezer's childhood was still multilingual. Even after the antiminority riots of 1955, Greek, Armenian, and Ladino could be heard in its streets. And even amongst confirmed and dedicated patriots like Tezer's parents, it was widely recognized that a child with mastery of at least one Western language would grow up to be of use in the nation's Westernizing project. It was this line of thinking that landed Tezer in Istanbul's Austrian lycée for girls. As much as she hated this school, it gave her German, opening the door not just to the great writers in that language but to all those whose works existed in German translation.

She does not say what of Pavese she first read in Turkish or if she first fell in love with his books in German translation. She might not have felt the need, for even in the Istanbul of her adult years, it was still not unusual to possess five or six languages, or to begin a sentence in one of them and finish it in another. But it was literature in translation, nevertheless, that freed her from her cold nights of childhood. Before Pavese came the Russians. With Pavese came the echoes of the many American authors—Steinbeck, Melville, Faulkner, and Dos Passos—whom he'd brought into Italian, breathing new air into his own work, and later, by osmosis, into hers. With her arrival into English, we might imagine a circle virtuously closed—were it not for a perhaps insoluble problem that this journey from language to language has brought with it across the better part of a century.

Journey to the Edge of Life contains forty-one quotations in italics and block text. A single footnote attached to the first quotation in the Turkish text attributes them all to Pavese. (Incorrectly, in this instance, as this first quotation comes from *An Absurd Vice*, the Pavese biography that sends Tezer on her quest.) In her German typescript, Tezer does sometimes indicate the letter, journal entry, or novel from which they came, if never the page number, but most are left unattributed. All of the quotations in the Turkish text seem to be her own translations of Pavese's German translations. As rusty as my German is, there is still enough left for me to notice a certain slippage between the German and the Turkish.

Without Italian, I had no way of measuring the German translations against the Italian texts. The only way forward, I decided, was to read as much of Pavese as I

TRANSLATOR'S NOTE

could find in English translation. Down the rabbit hole I went, and a very intriguing rabbit hole it proved to be, for I'd plunged in knowing next to nothing about Pavese. I crawled out many months later wanting to study Italian, if only to better understand his times, his generation, and the terrifyingly beautiful books whose English translations, where they exist, had rarely done them justice.

But I'd failed in my mission, as I'd located only half of the quotations. Those I'd found were mostly from translations from the mid-twentieth century that were either laughably awful or riddled with ancient slang and mistakes that even I, lacking Italian and only half remembering German, could identify. At the other end of the spectrum were two recent (and exceptionally wonderful) translations, both by Tim Parks. Taken together, it was hard to see the quotations I had located as coming from the same author.

What mattered most, I belatedly decided, was the meaning Tezer herself had taken from them. And that is why what you have read here are translations of what I found on the Turkish page, having also referred where possible to the German translations in her 1982 typescript and the English translations that were not conspicuously antique. In the footnotes that follow you will find an account of my investigations as far as they took me.

—Maureen Freely

Bibliography

Lajolo, Davide. *An Absurd Vice: A Biography of Cesare Pavese*. Translated by Mario and Mark Pietralunga. New York: New Directions, 1983.

Özlü, Tezer. *Yaşamın Ucuna Yolculuk*. Istanbul: YKY, 1984.

Pavese, Cesare. *The Beautiful Summer*. Translated by W. J. Strachan. London: Penguin, 2018.

Pavese, Cesare. *The Burning Brand: Diaries 1935–1950*. Translated by A. E. Murch and Jeanne Molli. New York: Walker and Company, 1961.

Pavese, Cesare. *The House on the Hill*. Translated by Tim Parks. London: Penguin Classics, 2021.

Pavese, Cesare. *The Moon and the Bonfires*. Translated by R. W. Flint. New York: New York Review Books Classics, 2002.

Pavese, Cesare. *The Political Prisoner*. Translated by W. J. Strachan. London: Peter Owen, 1955.

Pavese, Cesare. *The Selected Works of Cesare Pavese*. Translated by R. W. Flint. New York: New York Review Books Classics, 2001.

Endnotes

1. Davide Lajolo, *An Absurd Vice: A Biography of Cesare Pavese*, trans. Mario and Mark Pietralunga (New York: New Directions, 1983), 2. Retranslated by Maureen Freely.

2. Dylan Thomas, *The Poems of Dylan Thomas* (New York: New Directions, 2017).

3. Cesare Pavese, *The Burning Brand: Diaries 1935–1950*, trans. A. E. Murch and Jeanne Molli (New York: Walker and Company, 1961), 354. (Pavese's journal entry for July 14, 1950, written in English.)

4. Davide Lajolo, *An Absurd Vice*, 180. (Letter written to Francesca Pavese on August 30, 1942.) Retranslated by Maureen Freely.

5. Cesare Pavese, *The Political Prisoner*, trans. W. J. Strachan (London: Peter Owen, 1955). Retranslated by Maureen Freely.

6. Davide Lajolo, *An Absurd Vice*, 93. Retranslated by Maureen Freely.

7. "The Night" by Cesare Pavese, as quoted in Davide Lajolo, *An Absurd Vice*, 10. Retranslated by Maureen Freely.

8. "The Houses" by Cesare Pavese, as quoted in Davide Lajolo,

An Absurd Vice, 17. Retranslated by Maureen Freely.

9. Cesare Pavese, *The Political Prisoner*, 67. Retranslated by Maureen Freely.

10. Ibid., 99–100. Retranslated by Maureen Freely.

11. Cesare Pavese, *The House on the Hill*, trans. Tim Parks (London: Penguin Classics, 2021), 139. Retranslated by Maureen Freely.

12. Cesare Pavese, *The Moon and the Bonfires*, trans. R. W. Flint (New York: New York Review Books Classics, 2002), 10. Retranslated by Maureen Freely.

13. Ibid., 1. Retranslated by Maureen Freely.

14. Cesare Pavese, *The Burning Brand*, 325. Retranslated by Maureen Freely.

15. Davide Lajolo, *An Absurd Vice*, 242. Retranslated by Maureen Freely.

16. Ibid., 241. Retranslated by Maureen Freely.

TEZER ÖZLÜ (1943–1986) claimed her place in Turkish letters by breaking every rule imposed on her. Though she was dismissed by many and misunderstood by most throughout her short life, her writings have gone on to inspire a new generation of feminist writers and readers. *Cold Nights of Childhood*, her first book to be translated into English, won the National Book Critics Circle Gregg Barrios Book in Translation Prize.

MAUREEN FREELY grew up in Istanbul and now lives in England. The author of seven novels, and formerly the president and chair of English PEN, she has translated many Turkish classics as well as Orhan Pamuk. She teaches at the University of Warwick.

Transit Books is a nonprofit publisher of international and American literature, based in the San Francisco Bay Area. Founded in 2015, Transit Books is committed to the discovery and promotion of enduring works that carry readers across borders and communities. Visit us online to learn more about our forthcoming titles, events, and opportunities to support our mission.

TRANSITBOOKS.ORG